Delilah's Diary

JASINDA WILDER

This is a work of fiction. Names, characters, places, and incidents are either the product of the author's imagination or are used fictitiously. Any resemblance to actual events, places, organizations, or persons, whether living or dead, is entirely coincidental.

DELILAH'S DIARY

ISBN: 978-0-9882642-7-4
Copyright © 2013 by Jasinda Wilder

This book is for all the women who have had the courage to begin the journey.

Delilah's Diary 1: A Sexy Journey

June 7

I FOUND HARRY in *flagrante delicto* this morning. By which I mean, balls-deep in the church secretary, in our bed, in our house. Bitch had her varicose-vein legs all up around his waist and she was screaming, "Yes, yes, Harry, fuck me harder."

Just to clarify, Harry is my husband. And the church secretary is the pastor's wife.

I froze in the doorway of our bedroom, halted in the act of pulling my coffee-soaked sweater over my head. My tatas were sticking out of my too-small bra—too small because Harry was too much of a cheap-ass tightwad to buy me a new bra that actually fits—and my skirt was still soaking wet from the coffee I'd spilled on myself on the way to work, prompting my unexpected return home. My skin prickled into goosebumps, and I felt something hard and hot forming in the pit of my stomach.

I've always been a level-headed type of girl, not given to hysterics or outbursts. I've always done the *right* thing, the *smart* thing, the *good* thing. I saved myself for marriage, like a good girl. I only ever dated Harry, and we only ever kissed, on my parent's front porch, with my parents discreetly not watching from the living room.

Well, in that moment, with Harry staring at me with wide, frightened eyes over his sweaty shoulder...I lost it.

I mean, I went completely batshit crazy. I took off my stiletto heel and threw it at Harry, hitting Helen in the side as Harry tried to roll off her. She shrieked and toppled to the side and right off the bed, her floppy little titties bouncing as she fell. I took off my other heel and chucked it at my cheating-bastard husband as hard as I could. I nailed him right in the head. Cut open his forehead, loosing a ribbon of blood all across his naked, sweating belly and the clean white sheets, *my* sheets, my Michael Kors sheets I saved for a month to afford.

The shoe throwing wasn't the batshit part. That, I offer up, is a perfectly natural reaction to finding your pig of a husband porking a cheating whore of a homewrecker in *your* bed, on *your* Michael Kors sheets.

Yes, I was pretty hung up on the sheets.

No, the batshit part came later. Right then, after I'd hurled both shoes, I stormed past Harry into our walk-in closet and threw handfuls of clothes into the biggest suitcase I could find. I ripped dresses and skirts and blouses off the hangers, yanked piles of jeans and shorts off the shelves, and stuffed it all willy-nilly into the suitcase. I was still half-naked, wet and sweaty now, but I didn't care. Helen and Harry were watching me, silent, disbelieving, unspeaking, Harry pressing a hand to his gushing forehead.

I stripped my wet clothes off, only to realize I'd already shut the suitcase with all my other clothes in it, forcing me to dig, completely naked now, through the suitcase to find panties, a clean bra, and something to wear.

No one had said a word.

I hauled my heavy suitcase past the shell-shocked cheaters, not looking at them, not speaking to them. I grabbed my purse off the kitchen counter where I'd left it, stuffed my phone charger in my purse, and walked out.

Harry hadn't apologized, or tried to explain, and neither had Helen Warner. Suited me fine. What was there to say?

I got in my car, still unable to process thoughts through my raging, whirling, stunned head. I drove to the bank. My sister is the manager of the bank, and she's always hated Harry, for reasons I'd never understood. I stomped into the bank, into her office, interrupting a phone call.

"Betty, I'll have to call you back," Leah said into the phone, and hung up. "Delilah? What's wrong? What happened?"

I slammed the door behind me and collapsed into the chair in front of her desk. I didn't cry. I just sat there, staring blankly at the carpet between my feet.

"Dee? Talk to me. What's going on, honey?" Leah was beside me, kneeling with a hand on my knee, looking up at me with sincerity oozing from her pretty blue eyes.

I realized then that she knew. *She knew* about Harry and Helen Warner.

"Why didn't you tell me?" I said, the words a whisper.

"Tell you what?" She feigned confusion, but I could see worry lines forming between her perfectly-plucked eyebrows.

"About Harry and Helen." I dug my fingers into my trembling thighs. "I found them together. In *my* bed. *Fucking.*"

I never swore. I'd always considered cursing to be the sign of a weak mind, since that's what my parents always told me, but right then, a good strong curse word was all I could come up with.

"They were *fucking* in my bed, Leah. *Our* bed. My husband and the pastor's wife. In our bed." I leveled a glare at my sister, and it was vehement enough to send her stumbling backward, smoothing her silk skirt around her slim, perfect hips.

Her slim hips. Helen had *slim hips*. Like my sister Leah, Helen had small breasts, small buttocks, small feet and hands, small waist...

"You knew, didn't you?" I said. "You knew about Harry cheating on me."

Leah crossed around to sit at her desk. She straightened the legal pad and the pens, centering them, her eyes not meeting mine.

And then something else clicked into place. Looks exchanged during family dinners between my sister Leah and my husband Harry. A business trip I took to Chicago last fall, coincidentally occurring at the same time as Leah's husband was on a business trip as well. Now I was suspicious of Leah as well.

"Yes," she said, clicking a pen. "I knew. They've been sleeping together for months. Everyone knows."

Small town Illinois. Of course everyone would know, except me. Stupid, naive me.

Leah still wasn't looking at me, and that was when I knew for certain. She was guilty, and not just of forgetting to tell me about Helen. Leah's shoulders were slumped, her fingers trembling and tense.

I shouldered my purse, not to leave, but because it gave me something to do while I summoned the words to accuse my sister.

"You too, right?" It wasn't what I wanted to say, but it was a start. "You and him, on that business trip. You fucked him, didn't you?"

That word was coming easier, now. I liked it. It was a hard, dirty, sinful word. It made me feel less like a good little Christian girl, which I suddenly didn't want to be anymore.

A single tear dripped from Leah's nose to the calendar on her desk. She nodded. "When you and Mike both went on a business trip...Harry and I met in Peoria. Spent the week together. After you and Mike came back...there was just once more. After church one Sunday. You went home sick, and Mike got called into work."

"Does Mike know?"

I liked Mike. He was a genial, generous, kind-hearted man. He and Leah had two kids together, Lucy and Raymond. Good kids.

Leah shook her head. "No. It would kill him. His heart, you know. It's not so good these days." She looked at me for the first time in several minutes. Her mascara was running. "Please don't tell him," she whispered, hoarse, pleading.

"Who else—" My voice broke and tried again. "Who else has he fucked?"

Leah scrubbed her face, pulled a Kleenex from a box on her desk and dabbed at her eyes. "Cynthia Roberts. Tonya Hammond. That's all I know of for sure."

My head spun. "We've been married for *eight years*, Leah. Eight years. He's cheated on me with *four* different women? One of them my own *sister*?" I was close to yelling now.

"There's probably more. He's a dog, Dee. He always has been. Everyone saw it but you. Everyone knows Harry sleeps around on you."

He wasn't *that* good-looking, I didn't think. But then, ours was a small town, with a negligible supply of virile, halfway handsome men. Harry was tall, a little overweight now, but still carrying the natural bulk of powerful man. He was bigger than me, which was part of the reason I married him, honestly. He didn't make me feel big. I felt like a normal-sized woman with him. Helen had seemed tiny, in comparison. Like a doll underneath him. Leah, tiny little Leah…she must have been lost underneath him. The image slammed into my mind, and wouldn't leave: Harry, pale, hairy buttocks flashing and pumping, Leah, skinny, porcelain legs around his waist, tiny voice encouraging him…

I squeezed my eyes shut and tried to banish the image.

The hot, hard lump in my belly was moving upward now, lodged in my chest.

The same instinct that had driven me to pack up and leave was driving me now. I didn't second guess myself.

"Cash out my bank account, Leah."

Leah was startled by the sudden command, the steel in my voice. I've always been a meek person, despite my size. Leah was always the fierce, dominating one.

"But—but, Delilah...that's yours and Mike's... together. It's in his name too. I can't just—"

"*Now*, Leah. Or I'll tell everyone."

Everyone in town knowing a secret without it being said is one thing. Having it aired in public is another. Leah knew me well enough to know I had the means, as the editor-in-chief of the town newspaper, to spread the word if I wanted to.

Leah nodded. She tapped at her keyboard, and then scurried out of the office, summoning her calm-and-in-command face. I sat, seething on the inside and still on the outside. Leah returned with three fat envelopes. Twenty thousand dollars.

Harry and I had been saving for a down payment on a bigger house.

I took the envelopes and put them at the bottom of my purse, underneath the erotica novel I was secretly reading and my cell phone and my wallet.

"Good-bye, Leah."

I turned and walked out without a backward glance, leaving my sister, my only family, sitting stunned, and for once, speechless.

The bank was only a few blocks from the bus station, so I left my car with the keys on the seat, took my suitcase from the trunk and rolled it behind me. I felt eyes on me. People stopped in the act of eating their lunches at Loreen's Diner, in the act of getting in their cars, in the act of playing checkers in the park. They all watched me pull my overstuffed suitcase behind me, purse on my shoulder, eyes burning, to the bus station.

I couldn't take it. I stopped, turned to face the town.

"Harry Flores is a cheating *whore*!" I screamed, as loud as my lungs would go. "He's fucked half the town!"

I saw Cynthia and Tonya standing side by side on the sidewalk. Best friends, those two.

"Including you two, Cynthia Roberts and Tonya Hammond!" My voice was about to give out. "Including Helen Warner! And my *sister*!"

I turned back around, feeling the stunned, embarrassed silence close in around me. I refused to acknowledge anyone. I found the ticket counter, with hatchet-faced Marge Conyers behind it looking hard-pressed to meet my eyes.

"One-way ticket to Chicago, please."

Marge just nodded, punched the keyboard, handed me a ticket.

I turned away, then stopped. "You too, Marge? Did you fuck my husband?"

Marge turned eight shades of red. "Before you were married, just after he proposed." She wouldn't meet my eyes. "He's got a small penis, and he wasn't that good."

She looked surprised at that last, as if she hadn't meant to say it.

"I wouldn't know," I said, my voice cold and arch. "He's all I've ever had."

I found my bus, idling and about to leave. It was empty, but for a few stop-over passengers. I found a seat near the back and sat with my purse on my lap, fighting the burning in my eyes. The hot, hard lump was in my throat, now.

The bus rumbled to life and groaned away from the tiny town where I'd lived my entire life. I found the weight on my shoulders, which I hadn't noticed until that moment, lift away, leaving me better able to breathe. The more miles the Greyhound bus put between me and TinyTown, Illinois, the less weight I felt.

I made it an hour and half before the first tear dripped off my nose and onto my yoga pants. The only other passengers were near the front, several rows up, asleep or wearing earbuds. I let a sniffle out, and then another tear.

The storm swept over me, then, and I collapsed across the other seat, the armrest hard and biting into my side. I didn't care. I let the tears rip free from me, sobbing until I was exhausted.

When the storm passed, I levered myself into a sitting position again, and found an older black woman sitting in the seat across from me, eyes wide and brown and kind, gray-shot black hair tied back in a bun.

"Caught your man cheatin' didn'tcha?" Her voice was a gentle rasp.

I nodded, dabbing at my eyes with the hem of my triple-XL Disneyworld T-shirt.

"It ain't the end of the world, you know. Just the end of what you knew." She sidled across the aisle and sat next to me, took my clammy hand in her dry, papery one.

"What I knew *was* my world. He was my first, and my only. I saved myself for marriage, till I was twenty-one. I've never even kissed another man." The old woman just nodded and squeezed my hand, so I kept going. "We went to the same high school, the same college. I've known him my whole life. We dated for five years before he proposed, and in that time I never even *looked* at another man. I've been with Harry for thirteen years. Since I was sixteen. We barely kissed. On our wedding night, he—he got drunk, and so did I. I don't even remember...doing it. I remember it hurting a little, and then he fell asleep."

The old woman laughed. "Well, sweetheart, I hate to say it, but that may have been for the best. First times ain't what they're cracked up to be. My first time was damned awful. Course, he wasn't gentle, none."

"Harry was always gentle with me. Treated me right. Took care of me. But...it was always the same, with him. We'd get in bed, and he'd move up behind me and start touching my boobs. I'd... roll to my back, and he'd put it in, and then he'd finish, and that's it." I sniffled and looked out the window. "I'm sorry. I don't know why I'm telling you this. I don't even know your name."

"Susan," she said, giving my hand another squeeze. "You go ahead and tell me. You gotta tell someone, don't you? I been where you are."

"My name is Delilah," I said.

"Delilah. A pretty name for a pretty girl." Susan brushed a lock of my waist-length mouse-brown hair out of my eye. It was a grandmother's gesture, and it made me feel better.

"I spilled coffee on myself on the way to work this morning. Just a few hours ago. I went home to change, and I found him in our bed with the pastor's wife. She looked like she was enjoying it more than I ever did." My cell phone rang, and I shut it off.

"I found my husband just the same way. There was an accident at work, everyone got sent home. Came in to find him with my best friend. 'Course, he wasn't just doin' her. He was in her butthole. He tried to do that with me, once, but I wasn't havin' none of that." Susan shook her head. "He was my first, too, my husband. Wasn't my last though, and I came to find out what I'd been missin'. That's what you should do."

I looked at her in surprise. "In her...he was putting it in her butt?" I made a grimace of disgust. "Yuck. What do you mean, you found out what you'd been missing?"

Susan laughed. "Well, it sounds gross, but it's pretty nice, if he does it right." She gave me a serious, searching look. "You've had your world turned upside down, Delilah. You've left your home, and that's a good start. My advice? Just live life. Do things. Have an adventure. Meet a man and don't hold back. It doesn't have to be love, you know. It can just feel good, too."

Her words hit me hard. I wasn't sure if I wanted to believe her or not. What she was telling me went against everything I'd been brought up to believe in, all my life. I was a Bible-reading, church-going Christian. Sex was part of marriage, and an expression of love. Nothing else. Anything else was a sin, and an abomination before God.

Then her first admission filtered through. "Wait, you've done it...back there, with a man?"

Susan laughed uproariously, then leaned close. "Delilah, you just ain't got any idea what you're missing. There's a whole world waiting for you out there. Start with the simple stuff. Kiss a man, first. If you've never done anything but with your cheatin' ex-husband, then you gotta start simple. Go somewhere far away and figure out who you are. Just you start there. Find out who you are."

I talked with Susan all the rest of the way to Chicago. The last thing she said to me, before we parted ways on the platform, was life-changing.

"Delilah? Get a makeover. Change how you look. Go wild, girl. Who you used to be is gone. Be someone new."

She kissed my cheek, squeezed my hand, and walked away. I took my braid in my hand, my waist-length braid that had never been cut, and then looked down at my yoga pants and my tattered T-shirt, and realized Susan was right.

It was late afternoon by then, and I was alone in Chicago. I hadn't eaten anything that day, and I was getting shaky from hunger, so I took a taxi to a little restaurant I'd visited when I was here on my business trip, then found a room at the same hotel.

I stood in the bathroom of my hotel room after a shower, naked in front of the mirror, examining myself. My hair was nut-brown, loose, past my waist when unbraided. My eyes were a vivid cerulean, like sun-lit sapphires. Five-foot-seven, one-eighty on a good day. I touched my thirty-eight DD breasts, still perky but definitely heavy, with dark areolas the size of half-dollars, thick nipples. Wide hips, and a round but tight ass, always a little bigger than I'd like, no matter how hard I tried to make it shrink.

I ran my hands through my hair, which had never been truly cut in all my life, only trimmed an inch or two here and there. If I was going to get a makeover, it would start with my hair. Cutting it would be brutally difficult.

My skin was one of my best features, I'd always thought. Creamy and fair and flawless, soft as silk and white as porcelain. I ran my hands over my breasts, feeling a faint twinge of something electric deep in my belly as my palms whisked across my nipples. I'd heard women could pleasure themselves, but I'd never been brave enough to try. I mean, sure, I'd touched myself, learning my body as a little girl. But I knew without having to be outright told that to touch one's self like that was a sin, a dirty, worldly sin as bad as lying or stealing or using cuss words. As a young woman I'd hoped my boyfriend and then husband would provide the pleasure I wanted, and then when that didn't happen, I started to feel like to touch myself sexually would be cheating on my husband, and of course, there was the lingering stigma surrounding mastur-bation from childhood. I started a few times, when Harry was gone and I was desperate for any kind of pleasure in life, but I could never summon the courage to keep going.

Now, I slipped my hands down my sides and to my waist, running them down my full hips, and around to my thighs.

Should I? The idea of touching myself to feel sexual pleasure still made something deep in my psyche twitch with disapproval. Reason enough to try it. I was on a mission, I realized; I had to leave behind everything I used to be.

What better place to start than this?

I touched my breasts again, lifted them, then let them down and took a nipple between the thumb and forefinger of each hand, and squeezed, gently at first. Oh my…the electric current shot through me as I pinched myself, rippling down through my belly and into my knees, to my thighs and to my…

What should I call it?

I couldn't think of a word I liked. Vagina? No. I dismissed that one as too clinical. I thought of all the words I'd heard in movies, from the lips of the vulgar, read in my secret erotica novels—my one dirty little secret. Twat? Too foreign-sounding, too insulting. Cunt? *Hell* no; too filthy. Pussy? That was the word used in the erotica books the most.

I ran my hands down my belly and pushed my fingers into the triangular thicket of curly hairs. I liked that word.

"Pussy," I said the word out loud. It echoed in the small bathroom, an accusing sound. I said it again, pushing past the feelings of guilt and stigma.

"Pussy. I'm going to touch my pussy." I giggled. "Pussy, pussy, pussy."

I giggled again. Saying it so many times in a row made it sound like I was calling a cat.

I tried a sentence I'd read in my latest book: "I'm going to finger my pussy."

That sounded better.

I was blushing, though.

I put one hand on my breast...I adjusted my thought: my *tit*—and rolled the nipple between my fingers again, and then, just for variety, flicked it, quite hard. I gasped, and felt something dampen between my legs. It felt good. Very good.

I traced a finger along the crease of my pussy, still feeling a twinge of guilt at the nasty word. I wondered what it would feel like to put my finger inside. Would it feel like when Harry put his penis in it?

I felt nauseous thinking of Harry, so I pushed his name from my mind, resolving to never think about him again, unless I had no other choice.

Watching myself in the mirror, I put my hand over my pussy and dipped my middle finger into

my entrance, a slow, hesitating, exploratory swipe.
I felt wet, very wet, and warm, and—even to my
small finger—tight. An unwilling image of Harry's
penis flashed into my head, and I marveled that he'd
fit in there at all, without it hurting. I remembered
Marge's statement that Harry was small. What on
earth would a bigger man feel like? Would it hurt?
The times with Harry that I felt any pleasure at all
was when he took his time, went slow, rather than
just hump, grunt, and pass out. He would move
inside me, and the slippery sliding, the feeling of
being full...it was delightful, but it was always
over too soon, just as I began to feel something
building up inside my belly.

That pressure built now, way down deep, as I
toyed with my nipple. I slipped my middle finger in
again, as far as I could go, up to the knuckle. Oh,
that was nice. Very nice. It wasn't enough though.
Summoning my courage, I slipped my index finger
in with the middle one. Even better. Both fingers
dipped in, stroked the entrance and feathered
around the boundaries, touched the walls, and
then out and up to the keyhole-like area near the
very top. I found a little nub, a button. It was stiff,
almost like...like a penis in miniature. I touched it
with a tentative finger, and immediately my knees
buckled with a rush of intense sensation the likes
of which I'd never felt before, mind-blowing pleasure that had me reeling. With my knees trembling,

I gripped the edge of the sink, slipping in the water puddled beneath my feet and nearly fell.

Regaining my balance, I glanced over my shoulder at the bed, still made. I would be so much more comfortable doing this on by back, in bed. I laid down on the bed, still naked, and spread my knees apart, feeling wanton and sinful.

One touch to the little button had made me dizzy...what would it feel like to touch it until I simply couldn't bear it any longer? Time to find out. I knew what the fold of skin was, incidentally: my clitoris. I knew my anatomy, after all. I was hopelessly sheltered, not a complete moron. But knowing anatomy, or reading about the hero of an erotica novel "laving her aching clit with his tireless tongue" was a whole different story than masturbating for the first time at the age of twenty-nine.

I quested inward with my two brave fingers, touched my clitoris...my clit...again, and couldn't help gasping a little, just a quick intake of breath at the intensity of the feeling. More movement, then, a slow circle...oh God...why have I never done this before? The circle sped up, and then a wild pressure built up in the pit of my stomach, in the muscles of my legs and the small of my back. My hips began to flutter on their own, writhing me on the bed and lifting my spine clear of the mattress in an arch.

I heard myself gasping, nearly hysterical little whimpers escaping my lips as I began to move my fingers around my clit in a blur, and now fire was raging through my body and the pressure was expanding in an uncontainable whirlwind and I had to bite my lip to keep from screaming because my body was coming apart at the seams. I was frenzied, thrashing on the bed, hyperventilating, waves of pure intensity bursting through me, centered on the nexus of my pussy.

The waves became unbearable and my body turned hypersensitive, and I had to let myself go limp on the bed, panting raggedly. "Oh…my God…that was incredible." I was talking to the empty room, but I didn't care. If that was what I could do to myself, without really knowing what to do or how, then what could a man who knew how to give pleasure do to me?

The thought made me shiver, a shudder of anticipatory excitement, and not a little fear.

I fell asleep after that, exhausted from the day's events. I woke up in the late evening. I left the hotel, unsure where I was going or what I was going to do, but determined to do *something*. I wanted to start my life, and myself over. I was on a journey of self-discovery.

The thought struck me as cliché but true. My first inclination was to record the events as they happened. I'd kept a journal all the way through high school and college, and while I'd abandoned the habit in the wake of marriage and my career as a small-town journalist-turned-editor, I still found myself composing diary entries on my way to work, even though I never wrote them down.

I was a writer by trade. I'd majored in journalism because it had seemed a more viable way to make a living writing than with some nebulous dream of "being a writer." Now, with everything I knew gone and my future waiting to be written anew, I found myself not just wanting, but *needing* to start journaling again.

So I found the nearest place that sold electronics and bought a netbook. It's small, cheap, and portable, underpowered and low on memory but all I need for typing journal entries as I travel.

At some point between leaving home—or what had been home—and waking up that evening I'd decided I was going to travel, see the world. I had money, essentially stolen from my husband...soon-to-be *ex*-husband...and I was determined to make use of it.

I took my new netbook and sat down in a Starbucks to compose the preceding entry, sipping on a venti Chai tea latte. I might have cried as I began the words, just a few angry tears, but by the time I finished up to the asterisks a few paragraphs up, I was calm and ripping through the words at a furious pace.

I'm sitting there now, on my second Chai latte, not thinking about what's coming out of my fingers. People pass around me, chatter in twos and threes, read books and do homework and stare out the window listening to music. I'm surrounded by people but completely alone.

I don't mind the solitude. Back home...back *there*, there is no solitude. I was either at work or at home with Harry, or shopping, or visiting with Leah, or something. I was never alone, never able to sit and think and do whatever I wanted just *because*.

What do I want?

I want to live. I want to experience new things. I want to see Rome, and Athens, and Venice, and Paris, and London, and Tokyo and Turks and Cacaos. I want to feel a man's kiss, feel his hands doing *things* to me. I want to feel sex, and love. I want to feel desired. I want to feel alone in a foreign country. I want to feel brave, and yes, even afraid.

Until I caught Harry cheating on me, everything was the same: peaceful, boring, and predictable. I'd eventually have a kid with Harry, and I'd probably give up my position as an editor and my career in general to raise the child, and Harry and I would have sex on Saturdays and Sundays and I might never have known any different.

And then I spilled my coffee on myself. My life was thrown out the window, and my entire personality put into question.

I've never felt so alive before. I can do *anything*.

Holy shit, I'm terrified.

June 8

I woke up this morning ready for change. I looked up salons in the area and made an appointment for a cut-and-color later in the day. I'd brought all my clothes with me, but going through them, I realized they were all smart, savvy, no-nonsense business outfits, or comfy clothes. Nothing sexy, nothing fun. Nothing edgy.

I had breakfast and made plans. First step, new clothes. Hip, fun, sexy clothes. Next, find a lawyer and send Harry the divorce papers. I wasn't leaving Chicago until it was done. Then, buy an airplane ticket to somewhere far and exotic. Rome came to mind, once more.

Shopping for an all-new wardrobe turned out to be a lot more painful and difficult than I'd imagined. Things didn't fit, or didn't look right, or I couldn't figure what to pair it with or I just didn't think I could pull it off.

I stood in a changing room in a slinky red dress that cupped my curves and pushed up my breasts and showed off my legs…and I couldn't bring myself to leave the changing room with it on.

I asked myself, in no uncertain terms, what the hell my problem was.

Self-esteem. Harry had never been the type to compliment me, or tell me I looked beautiful. Sure, if I tried on a dress and asked him what he thought, he'd give me a stock response:

"Sure baby, looks great," he'd say, barely glancing up from his cell phone. "Makes your ass look nice."

And that was it. He'd grope me in the dark, before bed, and kiss me, a brief peck, on the way out the door, but nothing else. And he was *always* on his phone. He'd sleep with it under his pillow, stuff in his pocket when he was done sending a text or email. He would leave the room for sudden phone calls, send text messages surreptitiously. Now I realize how suspicious it all was, how clear. Then, I just shoved the fear away as paranoia.

But he didn't love me. Didn't want me. Why?

I wasn't beautiful. Wasn't desirable. He wanted a middle-aged, overweight, veiny, lumpy, floppy pastor's wife more than me. Sure, I was a little on the heavier, curvier side, but I'd thought I was at least better-looking than Helen *fucking* Warner.

Apparently not.

I left the second store in a row without buying anything and retreated to my comfort: blueberry muffins and Chai tea. I went back to Starbucks and got a latte and a muffin and had long sorry-fest until my appointment with the stylist, which I no longer felt like going through with. I forced myself to go anyway.

The stylist was an older woman, maybe fifty, fit and sleek and modern and all things cosmopolitan and lovely.

"What are we doing today, honey?" She asked me, fluffing her fingers through my long, thick brown locks.

I shrugged. "I don't know. A change, I guess."

She caught the depressed wistfulness in my voice. She paused with her fingers in my hair and met my gaze in the mirror. "Honey, I don't know you, but I know depressed when I see it, and can I just say that depressed is the worst time to get a haircut? Especially with hair like yours. You've been growing this your whole life, clearly. One moment of desperation, and it's gone. You can't get it back." She gave me a firm but kind smile. "I'm willing to do what you tell me, but I just don't want you to regret it."

I shook my head. "It's not that. It's a hell of a lot more than one moment of depression. My entire life is...changing. I'm changing."

I found myself once again pouring out my sob story to a complete stranger. I told her everything, and the dear woman—whose name turned out to be Julia—just nodded and listened and handed me a box of tissues. When I finished, she patted me on the shoulder.

"Honey, are you serious about really starting over?" She combed her fingers through my hair, a comforting motion. "No looking back, no changing your mind?"

I nodded, wiped my eyes and my nose. "I'll never go back there as long as I live. Not for my family, not for anything. I need to start over. I *have* to."

She smiled again. "Well then, if you're sure, I can start with your hair. I can think of a dozen things to do with a beautiful head of hair like yours."

I shrugged. "I don't know what I want. I've never done more than trim it. I've never thought about what I might look like with it cut." I thought back to my bout of self-pity in the dressing room. "I just...I want to feel new, and...beautiful."

Julia wiped a knuckle across her eye. "Oh, honey. Why do we let men do this to us? You *are* beautiful. I know it's hard to see it when they pull shit like this, but you can't give that bastard the power over your feelings. You are a strong, lovely woman, and I'll make you into someone new. I promise, you won't recognize yourself when I'm through with you."

I nodded, and summoned a smile. "Can you help me learn to dress like you, too?" I was joking, but only halfway.

Julia tilted her head. "You really are starting over, aren't you?"

"I stuffed everything I own into a suitcase. But then I realized those clothes are all the old me. Career and wife me. I wanted to buy some sexy new clothes, but..." I shrugged, going for nonchalant and failing, tearing up again. "I just don't know how. I've never been that girl."

"You don't just need a haircut, honey, you need a makeover. A total redo."

I nodded. "That's the plan, but I don't know where to start, except for this haircut."

Julia gave me an odd look. "Are you willing to trust me?"

I shrugged again—I seemed to be doing that a lot, suddenly. "Sure. I mean, I was willing to let you cut my hair off, so why not?"

She didn't answer, but pulled a cell phone from a drawer of her station and typed furiously on it.

"What are you doing," I asked.

"Calling in the cavalry," was Julia's cryptic response.

"That big of a job, huh?"

Julia rolled her eyes at me. "Honey, makeovers are always big jobs, and a true makeover requires a team. I'm just assembling mine. Still trust me?"

I nodded, my heart in my throat. I wasn't ready, but I never really would be.

The "cavalry" turned out to be two gay men, a couple, I assumed but wasn't positive. Their names were José and George, and they were both ridiculously handsome, in a polished, sophisticated, slightly effeminate way. José was Hispanic, maybe thirty, with sleek black hair, diamond earrings and a gold necklace showing between an unbuttoned silk shirt, wearing tight leather pants and custom leather shoes, rings on every finger, and piercing gray eyes. George was older, closer to forty or fifty, his head carefully shaved, a neatly-trimmed goatee framing a soft mouth, wearing a trim gray pinstripe suit with a faded designer T-shirt, pale blue eyes and long, slender fingers.

Julia gave them a Cliff's Notes version of what I'd told her, sparing me from having to repeat it, thankfully. José and George clucked their tongues and shook their heads.

George said, "Oh, sweetie. Men are such *dicks*, sometimes."

I agreed, and tried not to laugh at their sweet, genuine, affectedness. It was a contradiction in terms, it seemed to me, but true. They were at once completely genuine, but their mannerisms seemed almost put on, as if they wanted *everyone* to know they were gay, and how proud of it they were. I'd never felt my sheltered, small-town upbringing so poignantly until that moment. I felt judgmental and petty, trying to understand them, and failing. I couldn't figure out how to handle them, if I should treat them like men, or women, or both, or neither...they seemed to be a complex amalgam of both genders, somehow, and it made my head spin.

I stopped trying to figure them out when they started discussing tactics, as they called it. I couldn't keep pace. They were speaking their own language, talking about layering and matching the angles of my face and skin tone and eye color and...I just gave up and closed my eyes and enjoyed the sensation of hands in my hair.

I let them take me to a sink and wash my hair, the hot water relaxing my scalp and my frayed nerves. They toweled me as dry as my three footlong hair would go, and sat me down back in front of Julia's station.

"Are you ready, sweetie?" José asked.

I shrugged and nodded, a confused motion. José just laughed. He handed a pair of scissors to Julia and stepped aside with a flourish. Julia put the scissors to my hair, then stopped.

"Have you considered donating your hair?" She asked.

"I don't know. I didn't even know you could do that."

"Locks of Love would be able to make a great wig out of long, gorgeous hair like yours."

I shrugged yet again. "Sure, why not? If it's coming off anyway."

A few quick snips, and suddenly my entire upper body felt ten pounds lighter. I sobbed like a baby. José and George dabbed my face with Kleenex and told me how brave I was and how much I would love myself when they were done, and to just trust them.

"Sweetie, you are simply loveliness incarnate," George said. "And you deserve to see yourself that way."

I melted, and wished he was straight so I could kiss him.

I sat facing away from the mirror, with Julia's sure hands snipping and fluffing and snipping, until I was sure I would be bald when she was done, and then she did something with a foul-smelling concoction all over my hair and left me to sit and chat with José while she and George stepped outside for a smoke.

I told George everything. I wasn't sure why I kept pouring out my life's story to perfect strangers, but they all seemed interested and genuinely kind, and I couldn't stop myself. No one had ever really listened to me before, I realized.

"What you need," George said, "is an adventure. You need to go far away, and meet a man, and let him sweep you off your feet. Don't fall in love, though. Just let him make sweet love to you until you can't breathe. And then go somewhere else, and do it all over again."

José came in at that moment. "Don't confuse the poor dear," he said. "What she needs is a good fucking."

I blushed from my hairline to my toes.

" José, you rascal," George scolded, "can't you see you're upsetting her? She's not ready for that yet."

"I'm not upset," I said. "I'm just...not used to that kind of thing."

"Well that much is obvious." Geoge patted my knee, and then helped me stand up, escorting me to the sink once more. "Just take it one day, one step at a time. Trust your instincts, that's the first thing."

My hair was washed again, and dried, and then Julia spent a few minutes styling it before they brushed my shoulders off and unsnapped the apron.

"Close your eyes," George instructed.

I squeezed them shut, felt hands remove the apron from my shoulders and brush a few more bits of hair away.

"Are you ready to see the new Delilah Flores?" George asked. I nodded. "Well then, open your eyes."

I took a deep breath and opened my eyes. As promised, I didn't recognize myself. My hair had been waist length, wavy, plain brown, and not-quite glossy. Now it was pixie-short, above my ears, and bright, bottle-red, somewhere between crimson and maroon. It turned my features from seeming pretty enough but plain into...exotic and striking. My cerulean eyes stood out even more, and my porcelain skin seemed even whiter, even fairer.

My breath caught, and my eyes burned, even though I'd cried more tears than I'd thought one person could in one day.

"Well, sweetie? What do you think?" George asked.

I laughed and hiccupped. "I think I need a hug." I ran my fingers through my hair, a now alien sensation. "It's wonderful. I don't know what to say, what to think. It's...incredible. I don't know who I am."

"You're the new you," José said.

George gave him a disgusted look. "That has got to be one of the most idiotic things you've ever said, José."

I stood up and hugged José. "No, it's not. It makes perfect sense."

I found myself held close by all three of them, and the feeling of being embraced was enough to choke me up even more.

We broke apart, and Julia pushed me to the door. "Now go on. You have more makeover to do and I have appointments to keep." I pulled my wallet from my purse, but Julia stopped me. "No, honey. This one's on the house."

She handed me a business card. "This is my cousin. He's one of the top divorce attorneys in the city. I'll set up a meeting for you. He'll give you a good rate. Don't back down, okay?"

"Thanks, Julia." I hugged her again and followed José and George out the door.

They took me to Sephora and picked out a whole new array of makeup for me, giving me dizzying instructions on the proper use and application, only half of which I followed, not being big on makeup. Then they took me to Waterplace Tower Mall and the real fun began.

I don't know how long we spent there, browsing every woman's clothing store in the entire mall, sweeping through from front to back, examining every item on every rack. When I explained I wasn't concerned with a budget, their eyes lit up and they began pulling items like it was Christmas. They held blouses and skirts and wraps up to me, conferred in loud whispers about my "assets" and had me try on a thousand different outfits, pulling me out of the changing room with constant exhortation and encouragement.

When they first started yanking everything within three sizes off the racks, I'd wondered if maybe I should have set a limit, but I soon realized they really did know what they were doing and how to do it. For every six items I tried on, only one or two would make the cut, the rest being ruthlessly but gently put aside as "not what we're going for."

When we finished, as the mall was closing, I had spent almost four thousand dollars, but I had a whole new wardrobe of sleek, sexy items, designed to be interchangeable. We went back to my hotel room and I received lengthy discourse in fashion and accessorization, makeup application, and the importance of self-esteem.

Eventually, they dressed me in a knee length skirt, a sleeveless, low-cut blouse with a shrug over it, a tasteful necklace, low-heeled pumps, and tiny clutch purse with little more than some cash, my cell phone, and my wallet. I'd put the bulk of my money in the hotel safe, simply because it was too frightening to carry twenty thousand dollars on my person everywhere I went.

"Well, sweetie," George said, "you are officially made-over. How do you feel?"

"Better. On my way to being a new Delilah."

"Do you feel beautiful?" José asked.

I tipped my head from side to side. "Getting there. It will take time."

"Sure it will. But you have to believe it yourself, or no one else will. True beauty and style starts within, darling," George said. "Now, are you ready?"

I gave him a confused look. "Ready? I thought we were done?"

George laughed, a merry, belly-shaking chuckle. "To celebrate, of course! You can't get a makeover and not go out to celebrate. We're going to get you drunk and teach you how to catch a man."

José and George knew everyone, it seemed. I mean, literally everyone. They took me to a bar, more of a private club than anything else, really, the kind of place you had to *already know about* to know about. It was a wild, chaotic party, bustling with beautiful people all dressed to kill, swilling martinis and expensive wine and champagne with names I couldn't pronounce and top-shelf mixed drinks. Everyone was drinking, but no one was drunk. Everyone was paired off in some way, but everyone was checking out everyone else, gay, straight, or otherwise. It was crazy and confusing and exhilarating.

When I walked in, with José on one arm and George on the other, I immediately became the topic of frenzied whispers and excited conversation. I'd never in my life felt so many pairs of eyes scrutinizing me, examining me; not even when I'd lost my temper in the middle of Main Street the day before had I been so completely the center of attention.

I tugged my shrug closer around me, trying to cover the expanse of skin across my chest. I'd never worn anything so revealing before. I thought if I breathed too deep my nipples would pop out of my top, and I wasn't sure how I was going to sit down without flashing everyone.

"Why is everyone looking at me?" I whispered.

George answered. "Number one, because you look fabulous. And number two, because you're with us, and we're fabulous."

José chimed in. "Face it, Delilah. You're a sexy bitch. Get used to it."

I tried to contain my shock at being called a bitch. Where I came from, calling a woman a bitch was serious business; you just didn't do it unless you *really* meant it. I squeezed José's arm in thanks, because he'd clearly meant it as a compliment.

José and George—for some reason, whenever I thought of the pair, José's name always came first—dragged me to a bar and ordered a Tequila Sunrise, and then leaned against the bar, sipping their own drinks. They seemed to be waiting.

"Shouldn't we, like, mingle or something?" I asked.

George laughed. "No way, honey. We let them come to us."

I shrugged and sipped my drink, trying to go slow. I've never been a drinker. My parents weren't teetotalers, they were just heavy into moderation. I'd never in my life had more than three drinks, and that time, with Leah the day I graduated from college, I'd been dizzy and loud and completely not myself. I'd woken up with a pounding head and a vow to never repeat the experience.

José and George had other plans. They engaged me in intelligent, witty conversation, spanning everything from literature, which George was extremely well-versed in, to sports and politics and fashion. I wasn't aware of finishing my drink, but somehow ended up with a new one, and then we were surrounded by a dozen people and I was talking to a woman with ears pierced all the way from lobe to tip, hair shaved on the sides and long and braided down the center. She was a bartender and a film student, attending Columbia College. Then she vanished and I was being heavily flirted with by a huge, ravishingly handsome black man dressed in ripped jeans and a sleeveless T-shirt, showing off his rippling, ink-black biceps.

The man, whose name was Gerald, seemed to be trying to split me away from the group, edging towards me and gradually stepping into my personal space so that I was forced to back away from the group and the safety of José and George. My head was loose on my shoulders, and my thoughts slow. I'd had enough drinks slipped into my hands that I'd lost count, and suddenly I couldn't figure out how to extricate myself from the situation.

I glanced at George, whom I seemed to have connected with more than José. I tried to make "help me" eyes without Gerald noticing. I found Gerald handsome and charming, but his subtle manipulation of my personal space was intimidating, and I knew, in a cerebral and distracted sort of way, that I was in no condition to make any decisions.

"Delilah, dear, I have to visit the little boys room," George said, appearing beside me with a warm, firm hand around my wrist, "why don't you come with me?"

He didn't give me a chance to answer, dragging me away from an irritated Gerald. We made it to the bathrooms, and, to my shock, he went into the ladies room with me.

"George? Aren't you in the wrong, you know, bathroom?"

George just laughed and slipped into a stall. "Oh, honey. You're so innocent. Women always bring their gays with them into the bathroom. Girl talk, you know." He spoke over the sound of his urination, which made me blush.

He was such an odd combination. Some things about him were distinctly male, such as his direct, take-charge attitude and willingness to dart in and fix things. But then, after my initial shock, I really didn't feel too oddly about his being in a bathroom with me. Something about him, I wasn't sure what exactly, made my instincts recognize in him a nebulous sort of "one of the girls" factor.

I was also drunk, which might have had something to do with it. I peed, washed my hands, and fixed my makeup, under George's approving gaze.

"So Gerald was very...persistent," I said.

George sighed. "Yes, he is. He's a great guy, in some ways, but totally wrong for you. You did good getting clear of him. I have nothing negative to say about him of course, but he just isn't a good match for your stage in life."

"He kept pushing me out of the group, but he never touched me. It was weird."

"That's Gerald for you. He's very adept in social situations. You never notice him doing it, but suddenly he's got you exactly where he wants you: alone and susceptible to his many charms. He's done it to me before. It was fun, but...he's not my type."

I glanced at George as I put on a new layer of mascara. "You mean you and he..." George just nodded; now I was even more confused. "But he was flirting with me, and I'm a woman."

"He plays for both teams, sweetie." George seemed amused. "He's an equal opportunist, you might say."

I tried to digest being interested in men *and* women, but couldn't quite manage it. I shook my head and dismissed it.

"You should find someone you like, though," George said into my ear as we reentered the chaotic swirl of people and noise. "Don't go home with him, just...have some fun."

He led me back to the group by the bar, which had swollen by at least ten since we went to the bathroom. Gerald was nowhere to be seen, and there were a few men who looked, to my inexperienced eyes, to be straight enough to flirt with. But then, so had Gerald.

Good gravy, this was complicated.

George found a spot where he could keep an eye on me but still have his own conversations, effectively leaving me to own devices, but still somewhat supervised. I felt like a child on a leash, in a way, but it was comforting knowing I was being looked after. This was a difficult, confusing world I'd found myself in, and I was glad for someone to guide me through it.

I made small talk with a few people until I found myself chatting with a tall, gorgeous man with elegant clothes and an expensive haircut. I'd barely introduced myself when George sidled up to me.

"Honey, I haven't introduced you to Leon, have I?" George made a formal introduction. "Delilah Flores, this is Leon de Luca, a *very* good friend. Leon, this is Delilah. She's new in town."

Leon shook my hand, holding my fingers loosely, almost limply. I wondered, then, if George was steering me away subtly. Leon and George and I made idle conversation, until Leon made his exit and George rounded on me with an exasperated expression.

"Delilah, dear, have you no gaydar at all?" He asked in a harsh whisper.

"I guess not."

George laughed again, lighter now. "Well that much is obvious." He glanced around the room, and then pointed out a man with nice enough clothes and hair, but not the sophisticated elegance Leon had displayed. "See him? Is he gay or straight?"

I studied him. "Straight?"

George rolled his eyes. "No, honey. He's gayer than I am."

"There's different levels of gay?"

George burst into hysterical laughter, wiping his eyes with a prim finger. "Oh, God, honey, you have just no idea, do you? That's actually a fair question, but unimportant at the moment. See the way he's standing? All his weight is on one foot, his other barely touching the floor, with his hip popped out. Look at his arms, too, the way one is folded and he's gesturing while he talks with the other? Also, his clothes. They aren't expensive, but they fit him perfectly, and they're all precisely matched, from shoes to belt to watch. Now, that's not to say straight men can't dress nicely, but it's just not the same."

George scanned the crowd again, and this time pointed out a different man, taller, harder looking, with looser and more casual clothes.

"Now look at him," George said, pointing discreetly with one finger from around his drink.

"See the way his clothes are a little big? His jeans don't hug his ass, which is a nice one, by the way. And his nails are cut, but roughly. He's dreamy, but completely straight. Look at his stance. Feet apart, about shoulder width, one hand in his pocket and the other holding his beer."

I shook my head, amazed at George's eye for detail. "So should I flirt with him?"

George laughed again. "Honey, you're an adult. You can make your decisions on that. But yes, it's safe to flirt with him. I would, if he played for my team. I mean, god, honey, look at those arms!" He turned to leave, but then leaned close and whispered low in my ear. "If you do talk to him, don't, I repeat, *do not* say anything about why you came to Chicago. No personal drama. Keep it light and innocent. You're just here on business."

And with that, George sauntered off, leaving me with a half a drink and a fluttering heart.

The guy was hot. And now that George had pointed out the differences, I could see how you wouldn't be able to mistake him for anything but a heterosexual. By which I mean, all man. And for the record, his arms were *massive*.

I took a deep breath, summoned my courage, and made my way over to him. I had a rush of panic at the last second. What would I say? How did one strike up a conversation with someone you were interested in? My hands were trembling.

I was about to swerve aside when the man in question glanced at me, did a double take, and turned to face me. His eyes met mine, and I felt my breath catch. His eyes were a brilliant green, like wild grass in sunny field. His face was all angles and hard planes and symmetrical, rugged beauty, shadowed with a stubble of day-old beard. His jaw looked strong enough to break rocks on, and his hand clutching the beer seemed like a paw, big enough to make the beer bottle look tiny and fragile.

My heart went pitter patter when he pulled his hand out of his pocket and took a long step toward me.

"Hi, I'm Brad," he said, his voice like a bass drum.

His hand wrapped around mine, hard and calloused but gentle. He squeezed mine, firm but not crushing. I liked that. Most men either held your hand loosely, or crushed it. This was neither. His eyes locked on to mine, and seemed to twinkle with the promise of humor. Or something else.

"Delilah," I said, trying not to sound breathy.

I ignored my temptation to tug the shrug closer, and let him close the distance between us so we were standing just within personal space. His body radiated heat, and he smelled faintly of cologne and a scent I can only describe as clean male sweat.

"I haven't seen you around before, Delilah," Brad said.

"That's because I just got into town. I'm here on business." I kept George's warning in mind as I thought of what to say.

"Oh? What do you do?"

Not going to panic, not going to panic. No drama, no drama. I harangued myself and hesitated a beat too long. "I'm an editor. Of a newspaper. I'm in Chicago for a…workshop. For editors and journalists."

Brad nodded, and I realized this was my cue to ask him a question. Again, things were a few beats behind, making it awkward.

"So, Brad, what—what do you do?"

"I'm an architect." He seemed to sense my discomfort, and gestured at my now-empty drink. "Get you another?"

I nodded and followed him to the bar. George caught my eye and gave me an excited dou-ble-thumbs up. I made a face that was somewhere between excited and oh-shit. George just rolled his eyes and went back to his conversation with Leon, with whom he seemed to be flirting.

When we had drinks, mine a vodka tonic, now, Brad leaned close and gave me a relaxed, sexy grin. "So, if this is your first time in Chicago, how'd you end up here?" He waved a finger vaguely, meaning the little club we were in.

I thought hard, trying to find a way of explain-ing it that didn't involve getting into my complete makeover, which would then lead to my sudden flight to Chicago, which would lead to Harry, which would lead to me either getting angry or crying or both, which would be bad.

"Oh, I met them at a salon," I said, hoping I sounded casual.

Brad looked confused, and I realized what I'd said was a non sequitur.

"Sorry, I meant José and George. I came with José and George."

Brad made an "ah-hah" face. "Gotcha. They're good people."

"Yeah, they're great."

Awkward silence.

"So, how long are you in Chicago for?" Brad asked.

He was obviously trying hard to cover my blunders. I wasn't sure if he was attracted to me or not. He was leaning close, but it was loud in the bar. On the other hand, I'd caught his gaze wandering to my cleavage several times, so that might have meant something. But then, men did that anyway, so it might not. I told myself to stop over-thinking and just go with it.

"Oh, for a while. No set plans. We'll see."

Brad nodded, his brow furrowed. "So, you're in town 'for awhile', and you're here for 'business', and you just met José and George at a salon." He seemed to be leading up to something, so I stayed silent and let him continue. "You know what I think, Delilah?"

I tilted my head, heart pounding. Had I given something away? Said something wrong?

"I think you're running away from someone." He smiled, a wicked little grin that said he knew he was right.

I swallowed. "Is it that obvious?"

"Ha! I was right." Brad leaned a little closer. "I was guessing."

"How'd you know?"

His hand brushed up my arm as he set his beer down on the bar-top. "Your finger," he said, touching the line of whiter-than-white skin where my wedding band and engagement rings had been.

I traced the pale line myself, trying to keep my voice neutral. "So yeah, I guess you could say I'm running from someone. It's complicated." I backed away, expecting him to cut and run, now that he knew I had some kind of personal baggage.

He didn't though. "You know what you need? Tequila." He raised a hand to summon a bartender and ordered a pair of tequila shots.

He handed me one of the shot glasses and a wedge of lime. I wasn't going to admit it, but I had no idea what I was supposed to do with the lime. Then he took my hand in his, shook salt onto the web between my thumb and forefinger. I just stared blankly at him, and then the salt, and back to Brad.

He looked at me quizzically. "Never shot tequila before?"

I shook my head. "Nope. Let's just say I'm a little innocent when it comes to city life."

Brad chuckled, an amused rumble in his chest that made something in my belly tingle. The gleam in his eyes, a shine somewhere in between hunger, lust, and amusement, made my knees weak. I wasn't sure I was ready for what Brad obviously had in mind, but I wasn't willing to back out. Not yet.

"Well, innocent Delilah, you lick the salt, then you drink the tequila, then you suck the juice from the lime."

I shrugged and lifted my hand to my mouth, but Brad caught my wrist in his. "Not yet. We have to toast first." He didn't let go of my wrist. "To getting rid of exes."

He wiggled the fingers on his left hand; his ring finger had a similar white band where a ring had been. He lifted my hand to his mouth, never taking his vivid green eyes off mine, and licked the salt off my thumb, a slow, erotic swipe of his tongue. I blushed scarlet and a flicker of fire lit my belly.

"Your turn," he said, and tipped the shot glass to his mouth.

He'd already sprinkled salt on his hand. I took his hand in mine, realizing how huge his hand was, how strong, and lifted it to my mouth. My heart blasted in my chest, hammering so hard I thought he was certain to hear it, even over the music and laughter and voices. I ran my tongue along his hand, tasting the salty heat of his skin and then the sudden, powerful tang of the table salt, and then I had the shot glass to my lips and poured the clear liquid into my mouth. I swallowed it, and nearly sputtered it all over Brad, but managed to get it down. My face twisted into a grimace at the exotic, potent liquor, and then Brad shoved a lime into my mouth and I sucked it, the sweetly sour citrus dousing some of the fire in my mouth.

"Wow," I said, when I could breathe again. "That was...ahem...really something."

"It is, isn't it?" He was still holding my hand in his, and I wasn't pulling it away.

His fingers were playing along my wrist, tracing circles and patterns with the pads of his fingers around the inside, not quite tickling. I couldn't look away from his hypnotizing green eyes, and I felt a strange, fiery pressure in my belly, low, deep down where I'd felt it when I touched myself yesterday.

Then, the heat passed upwards, and something roiled in my belly, and I started to sweat, and get dizzy, and...

"I think I need some air," I said, trying to keep my feet steady underneath me.

"Ah, the shot must have hit you. Come on, I know a spot." He took my hand in his and led me through the crowd.

I felt another hand on my opposite elbow, and then George's voice cut through the dizzy fog.

"Where are you going, Delilah?" His voice was concerned, tinged with suspicion.

"I'm taking her outside to get some air," Brad said. "She did a shot with me, and now she's overheating."

I turned to George, and then to Brad, feeling wobbly. "I really need some air. I feel dizzy and hot. Sitting down would be nice." I glanced at George meaningfully. "Is that okay, George?"

I hoped he knew what I was asking, and that it wasn't too obvious.

Brad laughed. "George, you know me. Brad Mullins. I work with Uri. I'll take care of her, I promise."

George nodded and disappeared.

I glanced up at Brad, wondering if I'd insulted him. He seemed to be laughing still as he led me up a flight of stairs and out onto a roof. He sat me down on a bench and lowered himself next to me, his arm across the back of the bench but not exactly around my shoulders.

"I hope you don't think I—" I started.

"I'd rather you were suspicious than too trusting. Safer that way."

Now that I was outside in the cool night air, I felt better. Still a little too loose and too dizzy, but not sick anymore. I was intensely aware of how close Brad was, how near his huge arm was to me. I was stuck between wanting him to put his arm around me and being afraid.

I looked up at him, trying to gauge what he was thinking. His calm green eyes met mine, and I felt like he was assessing me too, not just my level of inebriation, but what I wanted.

What did I want? A kiss? That would be nice. A good place to start, perhaps.

I let myself lean a little nearer to him, closer to the curve of his arm. Brad adjusted ever so slightly, and then his arm was resting on my shoulders. It felt nice, hard and protective.

"Sorry to pull you away from all the fun," I said.

He shrugged a shoulder. "I needed some air too. Gets stuffy in there with that many people."

I just stared up at him, willing him to lean a little further. His face was only inches from mine, closer and getting closer, and my heart was thumping wildly...

His lips were softer than I'd thought they'd be, firm and scratchy with whiskers, but moist and hot and searching. He tasted like beer, not unpleasantly. My hand lifted up and rested on his shoulder, and his palm touched my face, pulling me nearer. This was nice. He wasn't pushing me to kiss harder or faster, wasn't groping me, just kissing me, slowly and gently.

Good gravy, the man knew how to kiss. Not that I had much by way of comparison, but... if Harry's and Brad's kisses were purses, Harry's would be an off-brand knock off from the bargain bin in K-Mart, the seams already ripping and the zipper stuck; Brad's kiss...oh my. His kiss would be a Louis Vuitton satchel bag.

I may or may not have moaned just a little, in the back of my throat.

"Wow, all I did was kiss you," Brad said, when we broke apart.

I flushed eight shades of vermilion. "Yeah, well...you're a really good kisser," I mumbled into his lips.

He smiled, a tight curve of lips against mine. "You are, too."

"What? No. You're just saying that." My fingers were somehow in his hair, and I was desperately fighting against the urge to pull him into another kiss.

"No, really." He touched his lips to mine, a teasing touch. "You taste like tequila, lipstick, and limes."

"Is that a good thing?"

"To me, yeah." He grinned. "I like tequila."

"It seems to be loosening my inhibitions a good bit," I said, smirking. "I mean, here I am, first day in Chicago, kissing a strange man on a rooftop."

"I'm not strange," Brad protested.

"I meant a stranger."

"I'm not a stranger, either. My name is Brad Mullins, I'm an architect, and I'm recently divorced. What else do you want to know?"

"I was teasing. I like being up here, kissing you. It's nice. It's a distraction."

His eyes bored into mine. "You need distraction?"

Don't talk drama, don't talk drama.

"Yeah, it's all still kind of...new." Shoot. Shit. I hadn't meant to say that.

"New?" Brad seemed concerned, suddenly. Now I'd done it.

Bye-bye, Brad.

"Don't worry about it. I'm here, now," I said, hoping to salvage things, if I could.

Brad's eyes narrowed. "How new?"

I slumped my head back against his arm. "Let's go back inside. I could use another drink."

I stood up, wobbling ever so slightly. Brad's hand shot out and touched my hip to steady me. His hand sent thrills of lightning through my body.

"I think maybe you should hold off on the drink," he said, standing up with me. "How about some coffee instead?"

"Do they serve coffee here?" I asked.

He laughed. "No, I meant get out of here, go get some coffee."

He wanted to *talk*. I just wanted to kiss a bit more, and then go home. Okay, maybe a lot more. But that was it. Just kiss. Certainly no talking. I'd told my story a million times in the last forty-eight hours, and I didn't want to rehash it all over again. Certainly not with a man I liked, and was kissing. Or had kissed. Or whatever.

"Sure," my mouth said, in spite of my brain's attempts at interference. "That sounds good."

He led me back downstairs and I found José and George huddled in a corner with two other men, looking very comfy and not a little flushed.

"Brad and I are going to go get some coffee," I said.

"Are you sure?" George said, pulling away from his friends. "You're okay?"

"Yeah, I'm fine. We're just going to have coffee."

"Okay," George said. "Just remember, don't do anything you don't want to do."

"I won't." I hugged George, and then José, who had appeared next to George. "Thanks, you two. I mean, seriously. Thank you so much. You don't even know."

George kissed me on the cheek, his palm circling my back. "Oh, honey. I *do* know. I've been where you are. Exactly where you are. José here did for me what we're doing for you. He helped me see who I really was." He wrapped his arm around

José's waist and pulled him close. "Just be true to who you *want* to be. Don't let anything hold you back. Now. Go have coffee with hunky Brad Mullins."

Coffee was a long, lazy conversation at an all-night diner, burnt coffee in chipped white porcelain mugs. Brad told me about his divorce, finding his ex in his bed with not just one man, but two. She got a better lawyer than he did and took every-thing, their high-rise condo, their savings, their car, everything.

I, in turn, told him my story. Helen Warner and her varicose legs, my sister, nearly every woman between the ages of twenty-one and fifty in the entire town. Taking the savings and running, the makeover, my vague plans of world travel.

"So this all happened like, days ago?" Brad asked.

"Yeah. I left on the ten a.m. bus yesterday morning."

Brad shook his head, amazed. "Well you're handling it a shit-load better than I did. I was a wreck for months. I mean, I got drunk and stayed drunk for a week straight. I almost lost my job until I finally went in and told my boss what had happened."

My mouth split open in a jaw-cracking yawn, and Brad pulled his cell phone from his pocket.

"Holy shit. It's past four in the morning. I should get you to your hotel."

He walked me to my hotel room door and we stood in front of it, hands touching, faces inches away. I let my body take over, leaned up to kiss him. He froze, then returned it, hesitantly at first, and then more eagerly. His hand moved to my waist and pulled me against him. Moments passed, and then more, and then my hands were running across his chest and in his hair...

I felt something hard bulging against my stomach, and it took a few seconds for the penny to drop.

And that's when the panic set in. Kissing a man, that was one thing. Touching his hair and feeling his arms around me, that was one thing. But his manhood...the idea of him naked in my room, touching me intimately...

I jerked free and fell back against the door.

"I'm sorry..." I said, touching my swollen lips with my fingertips. "I'm sorry, I can't...I can't."

Brad stepped closer to me, but stopped. I could see the bulge in his pants, pressing huge and hard against his zipper. My body and brain and hormones and heart were all at war, in a free-for-all.

"No, Delilah, I'm sorry. I shouldn't have—" he backed up, realizing where I was looking and interpreting, correctly in some ways, where my fear was concentrated. "I'm sorry. I'll go."

I grabbed his hand, not wanting him to think I was afraid of him, or upset with him. "Brad, listen...I'm sorry. I hope—I mean, I hope I didn't lead you to assume where this night was going...when it's not, or...it can't." I was flustered, stuttering; I ran my hands through my hair, surprised again at how short it was.

"You don't need to explain," Brad said. "I wasn't assuming anything. I mean, I hoped, in a way yes. But knowing how recent all this is for you...I wouldn't push it."

"I'm really sorry, Brad. I didn't mean to lead you on, or...or get you excited and leave you... uncomfortable. I'm just not ready." I was suddenly exhausted beyond comprehension. "I'm not even divorced yet. Shoot, I haven't even filed the papers."

"Don't apologize any more, Delilah. I understand. You don't need to explain." He kissed me, a gentle goodbye. "You're a beautiful, wonderful woman, Delilah, and your ex is an idiot."

He pulled a card from his wallet and handed it to me. "If you ever want some company—no expectations—call me."

He backed away, and I, under a wild impulse, darted forward and kissed him again, quick but hot.

"Thank you for understanding." I said.

He smiled, waved, and was gone, pushing through the crash bar to the stairs.

I pulled out my keycard and went into my room, collapsed on my bed and tried to figure out if I'd just made a mistake in letting Brad go, or if it had been the smart thing to do. My brain argued one way, my heart another, and my body a third.

I fell asleep, still arguing with myself, cross-wise on the bed.

June 11

The last several days have been a whirlwind. I went through the process to get my passport, and I met with Julia's divorce attorney cousin, who drew up papers and sent them by overnight to Harry. I'd been honest about clearing out the savings account. The lawyer suggested giving Harry everything else, the cars, the house, the stocks and investments, everything. I agreed. I just wanted to be done.

Harry signed and sent the papers back in an overnight priority mail. A weight lifted off my shoulders and I could breathe again. Or maybe, breathe for the first time. I was a single woman again. I spent a day at a spa to celebrate, getting a facial and a mani-pedi, a massage and all sorts of other indulgent pleasures.

I went to a travel agency and looked at travel packages, but they all came in groups, with hour-by-hour itineraries and all sorts of premade sight-seeing tours. I wanted something loose and personal and free. No plans, no groups, no tours. No itinerary, just me, out there.

I donated all my old clothes, packed my new wardrobe in a new set of overpriced luggage and bought a one-way ticket to Rome, Italy. I don't know a word of Italian. I've never been out of the country. I don't have a hotel booked, and I don't know anyone.

I'm terrified and exhilarated.

The plane is about to land at the Leonardo da Vinci-Fiumicino International Airport. I have my purse with a bundle of cash, and the rest split between my carry-on bag and the suitcase. I didn't want it all in one place, and I don't know a better way. Traveler's checks? I don't know. I'll learn, I guess.

June 12

Today was crazy. I spent an hour just trying to get out of the airport. I bought an Italian-English dictionary, and then realized the Google Translate app on my iPhone is much more effective. I can just plug in the phrase I want in English, have the app translate it into Italian and show it to the person I'm trying to communicate with. That's how I got a security guard to show me the way to the taxi line, and then found a mid-grade hotel in what I take to be the center of the city.

OHMYGOD. Rome is incredible. Age and history oozes from every brick, every cobblestone. Even the more modern buildings are older than pretty much everything in the US.

I stowed my purse in the suitcase and left it in my hotel room, putting what I need to travel in my backpack and my pockets. I wandered around in an awed daze, taking in the many famous sights of one of Earth's oldest and most storied cities. It's dirty in places, tumbledown, ramshackle, haphazard. It's rough, and difficult. It's beautiful.

I walked until my feet hurt and then showed my hotel's business card to a taxi driver, who answered in clear but heavily accented English, "Yes, ma'am. Right away, ma'am. You need to eat some food, maybe? You are hungry, no? Too much walking? I take you to a great place. My cousin, he cooks the best pasta in all of Roma. You will die of loving the food, I swear you this. Wine and good food, you will be like new, no?"

I let him take me to his cousin's place, which turned out to be a few blocks from my hotel, and the food was divine. I'm sitting outside, sipping red wine, clacking into my netbook, watching crowds go by, tourists and locals. Soccer, or I guess I should call it football, is on a TV and the locals clamor as goals are scored, groan as the opposing team scores back.

I'm free. I'm happy. Anything can happen. I promise myself, as I write this, that I will not let opportunity pass me by. Fear cannot stop me, not anymore. I will let life sweep me away. I have a good head on my shoulders, a sense of right and wrong.

June 13

Today I met Luca. Oh, lord. Luca. How do I describe him? Just saying his name is like music, like poetry. Luca.

Tall, dark, and handsome doesn't even begin to cut it. A physical description won't do him justice, because he's male beauty personified, but I'll try.

Six foot three or four, lean and hard with broad shoulders and a slim waist, long, thick legs. Inky, glossy black hair, a little too long, a little messy, drifting in front of his eyes, and oh, his eyes. Good gravy. Luca's eyes are the brown of...what? Cinnamon and melted milk chocolate. Rich, dark earth, lit by the sun. His hands are powerful, but gentle. Long fingers, musician's fingers, nimble and sure.

Every word from his mouth is lyric, lovely music.

He says my name like it's a song: "Dee-LYE-lah."

Let me go back and tell the story from the beginning, get it right. Luca is best understood in the context of how I met him.

I was sitting on the ledge of fountain, digging through my backpack for sunscreen. I spread the sunscreen on, tossed it back in the open bag and leaned back, enjoying the heat of the sun on my face, the sound of splashing water and laughing conversations. It was late afternoon, not quite time for dinner, but well past lunch. The sun was lowering, shedding soft but bright golden light on everything, illuminating the aged marble of the millennia-old buildings.

I let my mind wander, imagining Roman senators crossing this very spot. Cicero, maybe. Or Pliny. Or was Pliny Greek? I couldn't remember at the moment and didn't care.

Then I heard slapping feet and a sound as of something heavy being snatched, and the breeze of someone running past me. I opened my eyes to see a young boy scrambling through the crowded piazza, my backpack in hand, open, spilling things out as he ran.

My backpack. Shit! That bag had several thousand dollars in it, and my passport, and my netbook...

I cursed and took off after him, thankful that I'd worn sensible sneakers. He was fast, the little shit. I followed him through alleys and narrow side streets, nearly catching him, only to lose him as he leapt over a crate of oranges that I tripped over, scattering fruit and earning an earful of Italian curses.

I scrambled to my feet, yelling an out-of-breath *"Mi scusi, mi dispiace!"*

Yeah, I've learned a little Italian.

I caught sight of the little thief rounding a corner, pulling away from me, and I heard sobs scrape out of my throat.

"No, please," I gasped, stretching out my arm as he began to move out of sight.

Then, a miracle. The boy turned back to look at me, almost apologetically. He didn't slow, but he seemed to realize how distraught I was. He turned back around, poured on more speed....and then a body shot out from a doorway, knocking the boy against a wall and held him there with one hand.

Hello, tall, dark, and handsome. He was holding a cell phone to his ear, talking into it in lilting, rapid Italian, holding the runaway thief against the wall with the other hand. His grip on the boy's shoulder was obviously crushing, as the boy was squirming and shrieking, scrabbling at the man's hand with both of his, my backpack dropped at his feet.

(I've since learned enough Italian to be able to guess what they were saying. For the sake of storytelling, I'll transcribe their words in Italian, as I heard them, in other words, un-translated and confusing.)

"Lasciatemi andare! Mi dispiace! Non farmi del male! Lo darò indietro!" The boy's voice was high-pitched, panicked.

"*Dovrò richiamare*," The man said into the phone, then hung up and stuck it into the pocket of his tight jeans. "*Zitto, ragazzo*," he said in a harsh voice, shaking the thief.

I hurried to them, snatched up my bag and made sure the important things were all there, which they were. The boy was looking as if the man was really hurting him, and I felt bad for him. He was skinny and dirty and hungry-looking, desperate.

"Let him go," I said, in English. "I have my bag back. Don't hurt him."

"Tell the American lady you're sorry," the man said, in accented English.

"Sorry! I'm sorry, American! I only am hungry. *Mi dispiace!* Please, let go!"

The man shook the boy once more, then let go, shoving him away, growling in accented but fluent English, "Get out of here, boy. If I catch you stealing again, I'll turn you over to the police."

The boy nodded, pale and shaking, and vanished around a corner. I zipped my bag and shrugged it on, then looked up and found myself pinned to the wall by the most arresting pair of dark brown eyes I'd ever seen. He didn't just look at me, he seemed to be looking *into* me. Seeing all of me, as if I were naked before him, vulnerable and soft.

My breath caught, and I couldn't look away. I felt strong fingers touch my palms, scraped from my fall.

"You are bleeding," he said, his voice and accent turning even those mundane words into music.

"I'm...fine," I said. My hand was still in his, his touch like fire, sending thrills through my body. "Just a scrape..."

"No, you need care. Your knees are a mess as well. Come, please come." He tugged me by the hand, gentle but insistent. "My flat is just there. I can have you cleaned up in only a moment."

I looked down and realized my knees were oozing blood too. And now, suddenly, they stung. And I was sweating...

I let him show me up a narrow flight of steep stairs to an airy one-room apartment. It was clean and neat, a galley kitchen, a small balcony overlooking the street, a small table covered by a white linen cloth and an empty wine bottle turned into a candle.

"Sit, please," he said, pushing me into a chair.

He wet the corner of a towel and dabbed at my hands, kneeling between my knees. His presence was a hot, electric fire in my veins, his inky hair drifting across his eyes, his brow furrowed as he *oh so gently* dabbed at my palms, then each knee.

"There, you are clean now. You want a bandage or no?" he asked.

"No, I'm fine, thanks," I said.

What I wanted was for him to keep touching me. Just his hands on mine, or on my knees would be fine. A littler higher up my legs, maybe?

He pulled the other chair next to me, sitting astride it, resting his hands on the back. "So, *mia bella*, what is your name?"

Mia bella? I knew enough Italian to know that was a compliment, and to flush crimson.

"Delilah," I said, holding out my hand to shake his.

He took my proffered hand and kissed the back of it, never taking his eyes off mine. His lips on my hand burned like fire, sending shivers of delight up my arm to coil hot and heavy in my belly. He'd actually kissed my hand. I could barely think, for a moment.

"I am Luca," he said, after I failed to ask.

"Oh, sorry, yes, I was going to ask but I... you..." I stopped, took a deep breath and gathered my composure. "It's a pleasure to meet you, Luca. Thank you so much for getting my bag back, and taking care of me."

Luca smiled, his straight white teeth brilliant against his dark olive skin. "The pleasure is all mine, Delilah."

"I don't know what I would have done if I'd lost my bag. It has everything in it."

"Roma can be most dangerous, at times. You are here alone?"

I nodded. "It's a beautiful city. I've always wanted to see Rome."

"Is it what you thought it would be?" Luca asked, resting his chin on his hands along the back of the chair.

"Yes and no. In some ways it's so much more than I'd ever dreamed, but in others…"

"It is not so lovely in some ways, too, no? I know this. I am from…you call it Florence, I think…and I too am often surprised at the state of things here in Roma. It is a complex place. You should see Firenze. *Mio Dios.* So lovely." He gave me a quirky smile, roguish and cunning. "So lovely, like you, Delilah. The only thing Firenze needs to be perfect is you, walking her streets."

I think I melted, right then. All I could do was blush redder and look away, down at the cracked and faded tiles beneath my feet. Was he trying to give me a heart attack? Was he really talking about me?

"I'd like to see Florence…what'd you call it? Firenz?"

He laughed, a flash of white teeth and kind mirth. "No no no. Firenz-EH. with the 'eh' on the end. Firenze. Florence is the English word. We call it Firenze."

I tried the Italian pronunciation, giving it the lilting accent he did. "Firenze…it's much lovelier that way. But yes, I think maybe I'll see Flore—Firenze next."

"For how long are you in Roma?" He grinned again. "That's how we say 'Rome' by the way. *Roma.*"

"I suppose I should have learned some Italian before I came, huh?" I laughed somewhat sheepishly. "I don't have any definite plans."

"Well, you are learning now, no? I am a good teacher, I think. I will teach you more. For example, 'thank you' is *grazie.*"

"That was the first thing I learned. And 'thank you' is *per favore.*" I showed him my phone, and the app I'd been using to translate. "I've learned a few phrases with this."

Luca laughed again, waving his hand in dismissal. "Bah. Technology is a wonderful thing, but I think perhaps nothing is so good as a person to teach you a language. There are many small things to speaking truly that no program or app can ever teach." He stood up and extended his hand. "I think maybe after so much running you are hungry, yes? Eat with me, Delilah."

There was no hesitation. I took his hand and let him draw me to my feet. "I would like that."

We walked through the streets of Rome, or Roma, I should say, him guiding me with subtle nudges. He worked for a vineyard, selling cases of wine to restaurants and bars throughout Italy and some of the surrounding countries. He was the youngest of four children, all of whom except him lived and worked in Firenze, a stone's throw from their parents. Luca traveled much of the time, but still spent a few weeks at a time with his family, "on holiday" he called it.

We sat across from each other in a little cafe, from which I could see the huge gray bulk of the Coliseum.

"I am returning to Firenze tomorrow, actually. I have been in Roma for a week, working, and for three months before that traveling in the north. I am ready to go home and eat my mother's cooking." He grinned. "I am what you Americans call 'a mama's boy'. I am not ashamed of this. My mother makes the best food in all of Italy, I think."

"I think it's sweet that you're close to your mother," I said, sipping the wine he'd ordered, something dry and unpronounceable and delicious.

"Europeans are often much closer to our families, I think. I have traveled in America a few times, and I think this is true."

"I think you're right," I said. "We move away when we're old enough, and it gets hard to travel back home. It's at least partially because America is just so big."

"It is also a matter of culture, and the raising of children, too," Luca said. "Not to mean that

Americans do not love family, but for us it is different, I believe."

I let Luca order for me, and we ate slowly, enjoying each bite, trading stories of childhood. I'd managed to avoid any discussion of my reason for coming to Italy thus far, and I was proud of it. Don't talk drama, George had told me.

"So, why have you come to Italy? Just for vacation?" Luca had a sly look on his face, as if he knew differently. "I think it is more. You are alone here, yes? No friends, no husband, no travel group?"

I hesitated, wondering what to say. Eventually I decided on some of the truth. "Yes, I'm alone. I just had to get away from everything for a while, and the thought of going with a bunch of random strangers, just seeing a few tourist-y spots and moving on...no, thanks."

"What is it you are getting away from?"

I shrugged, trying for casualness I didn't feel; it was still a sore spot. "Just...you know. Life, drama. The usual."

Luca waved his fork. "Ah. Drama, this I know. Perhaps you do not wish to discuss it, I think. You are on holiday to forget, no?" Our waiter brought dessert, spumoni for each of us. "Ah, now this looks delicious. You have had spumoni before?"

And with that he was off again, the topic mercifully changed to our favorite desserts.

When we finished, Luca paid, refusing to let me contribute, and we walked again, strolling aimlessly. Night fell gradually, time slipping away beneath our feet. We rested now and then, sitting on benches, our conversation endless and naturally flowing from topic to topic. Luca was careful to keep our conversation away from anything serious. Eventually we ended up on a high hill overlooking the city, leaning back against an ancient stone wall. We were sitting close enough that our shoulders and thighs touched, and with every brush of clothed flesh I felt a current of electricity buzz through me. I wished, like a school girl, that I was brave enough to kiss him, or even hold his hand.

"I leave for home tomorrow," Luca said, apropos of nothing. "I was thinking...perhaps you might like to travel with me? It would be a free ride to Firenze, after all, and if you did not mind my boring company on the way..."

My heart leapt into my throat. "I...you aren't boring, Luca. Just the opposite." I was thinking, frantic as a lovesick teenager, *he likes me, he likes me, he likes me!* "I would love to, thank you."

We wended our lazy way back to my hotel, and Luca stood with me outside my door. My heart was hammering in my chest, although I wasn't sure why.

I'm going to kiss him, I realized. My nerves knew before I did.

My back was to my door, Luca standing in front of me, one hand planted next to my head. We weren't speaking, for the first time in hours, just staring at each other. I was waiting for him to kiss me, wondering if he would, wondering if I should make the first move or if that would be offensive.

"I would like to kiss you, Delilah," Luca whispered, interrupting my thoughts. His voice was a breath on the breeze.

I tilted my head up, lips parted, and then my hand was in the feather-soft black locks by his neck and our lips were touching, barely grazing at first and then with more urgency.

He tasted so good, like wine and heat. His feet moved to bracket mine, and his hands were on my waist, and then one moved up to brush my cheek and slip past my ear into my hair. His hard body pushed up against mine, and I could feel the faint thump of his heart in his chest, a little fast, as if he was nervous too. Surely he could feel mine, hammering in my chest? I was terrified. I wanted this to continue, I wanted the kiss to last forever and never change, but I wanted more, and he was so hot, so sexy, and he was kissing me, *me*, Delilah Flores.

His hand moved around my waist to my back and slipped down, stopping mere centimeters from caressing my backside, and I really, *really* wouldn't have minded if he kept going.

"Perhaps we could move to the other side of the door?" Luca suggested, a smile in his voice.

I nodded, unthinking, letting my instincts move me rather than my fears or inhibitions. I fumbled in my bag for the key, found it, managed to turn away from his molten, desire-sparking eyes long enough to unlock the door and get inside.

Something exploded in my belly then, burst apart my fears. Luca closed the door and turned back to face me. I might have attacked him, just a little. A wave of pure lust ran through me, demolishing everything but desire. He was here, in my hotel room, larger than life, hair tangled across one eye, jeans low on his hips and tight around his firm ass. I wanted to touch him all over, feel him pressed against me, let him take control and float along for the ride.

He caught me, let me crash into him and crushed his lips to mine, and now—oh God—his hand slipped down my spine to cup my bottom and pull my hips against his.

Damp heat blossomed between my thighs, and I sighed into his lips.

"I like this," I said. I hadn't meant to speak, but the words dripped out of my mouth unbidden.

Luca laughed, a huff of breath against my lips, a smile curving his luscious mouth. "That is good. I like it as well." He moved his other hand to my backside, curling his fingers into the muscles beneath the fabric of my knee-length skirt. "Do you like this, as well?"

I nodded, and let my hands find their slow but eager way to his chest, feeling the bunched muscles. It wasn't enough, though. My hands wanted more. They wanted to feel hot skin. They snaked underneath the thin fabric of his T-shirt and skimmed his stomach, lightly brushing the dusting of hair to rest on his chest again.

He smirked, and then mirrored my action, slipping under my shirt and running up the skin of my back, coming to rest just beneath my bra strap. I gasped at the contact of skin to skin, pressed up against him and curved my hands around to touch his back. He just lifted an eyebrow, and kept still. Was he playing a game?

I lowered my hands down the ridges of his spine and the hard creases of muscle along his back. Now I was touching him just above the waistband of his jeans.

Dare I?

Oh, yes, I dared.

I moved my hands under the jeans and his underwear to clutch the cool hardness of his backside. God, it was like rock. My heart was a tympani beneath my ribcage, thundering wildly. Would he reciprocate? Would I die when he did?

His thumbs brushed the outside of my thighs, hooked under the hem of my skirt and lifted, pressed his palms to my lace-clad backside. His eyes were locked on mine, waiting for me to tell him no, but I kept silent, willing my heart to slow. It didn't, and when I didn't demure, but kept my eyes bold on his, he slid his hands under the lace to my bare skin.

I trembled, sucked in a deep breath at the buzzing thrill of strong, desirous male hands on me.

"You are okay, Delilah? I do not wish to press you, if you are not wanting this as I am." I could only nod, and he tilted his head. "You are nervous, then."

I nodded again, but knew I had to say something, this time. "Yeah, I'm nervous. It's...it's been a while. But I don't want to stop."

"You will tell me if I move too fast, okay?" he said.

My panties were pink lace, lingerie I'd indulged in for fun before I left Chicago, and was wearing them because they made me feel sexy and daring. Would he see them? The thought of standing in my bra and panties in front of a man was scary. I'd never done it before. That's not how things were with Harry. We had sex in bed, with the lights out. I'd never stood before a man in any state of undress, not intentionally. Oh, sure, Harry saw me naked all the time, just out of the shower, or changing, but...

God, as I write this I realize the hard truth: Harry didn't want me. He didn't desire me. I was safe, for him. I was security. I had a career path and I took care of him. But sexually, I was just there. Available, but not his preference.

Luca...he *wanted* me. It was in his eyes, in the roving possession of his hand, the bump of his hips against mine. His desire was infectious, and intoxicating.

I'd never been desired before.

I needed to show Luca that I wanted him too. I brushed my hands up his torso, along his sides, and lifted his shirt off. Holy hell and good gravy. His body was chiseled from flesh-covered granite. My lips, of their own free will, touched his shoulder, an inch away from his neck, and then closed in to where his throat met his clavicle, and then to his adam's apple.

I'd never kissed a man, thus, with such tender passion. I didn't love Luca, but I *wanted* him, in a way I'd never wanted anyone.

Luca kissed my temple, feathered his fingers through my hair as I paid oral homage to the temple of his body, then skimmed his hands up my back and lifted my shirt free, and my thudding heart went mad.

"Your heart, it is beating so hard," Luca laughed. He tipped my chin up to look at him. "You are not only nervous, I think. You are afraid. Am I scaring you, Delilah?"

I shook my head, then nodded, and then laughed at my indecision, sniffling. I wasn't crying. I wasn't.

Shit. Yes I was.

(Cursing comes easier with every passing day; in writing, it is even easier. No one will ever read this diary.)

"Delilah? *Mio dios*, you are crying. It was too much, I knew it." He sat me down on my bed, pulled me against his chest.

I was in my skirt and bra, but he hadn't so much as peeked at me yet. This just made me cry harder.

"I'm sorry, Luca," I whispered, choking back the crazy, unwelcome, confused tears. "It's not you. I don't know what it is. I was enjoying it, really I was. I don't want to stop. I don't know why I am crying."

"Tell me, *mia bella*. What is it you are trying to forget?"

I shook my head. "No. No drama." I wiped my eyes, took shallow shuddering breaths.

And then Luca, sweet, sexy Luca, he kissed my hair line, and then my temple, and then my cheekbone, and then my jaw, and it was as if I'd always known him, always felt his kisses on my face. So familiar, so foreign; so electric, so comforting.

It only made another tear track down my face, and then I was talking. Again. Telling my stupid story, again. I had it down to a quick run-through at this point, an almost memorized patter of the facts: small town girl married her high school sweetheart, found him cheating on her and left him.

"But then why are you so afraid of this?" Luca asked. "You are not a virgin, it is not your first time, nor mine. I am not hurting you, am I? Not giving you pressure to do this?"

"No! Like I said, it's not you, not in any way. It's just...Harry, my ex-husband, was the only one I've ever been with. And with him, it was always in bed, in the dark. Once we were married—and we waited until we were married for our first time, or I did, at least—there wasn't much romance to it. We barely kissed. He didn't touch me like you are. He just...did what he did, finished, and went to sleep." I couldn't look at Luca as I said this. "I don't know what I'm doing. I don't know any-thing, except that...I want you. I want this. You... you look at me, touch me like you actually want me, and it—it's so wonderful. But yeah, I'm scared. It's new, and I feel vulnerable. What if I'm bad at it? What if you don't like...it...with me? It's like I *am* a virgin, in a way. In terms of experience, I mean. I've never done anything. I just let Harry do what he wanted, and that was it."

Luca's eyes were burning, with anger, but not at me, I didn't think. "Oh, Delilah. You poor girl.

You have been so ill treated. That is not love, that is not even really sex. This Harry was only a selfish pig of a man who did not deserve you. You need to be taught what true pleasure is, I think." He tipped my chin up and kissed me, ever so gently. "If you are sure you want this, with me, tonight, I will be as slow an educator in the arts of love as you could wish. If not, there is always another night, and do not think I will be upset, please."

Yes, Luca really said that. He wanted to educate me in the *arts of love*? Oh, Venus, still my beating heart.

"Answer me, *mia bella* Delilah." His command was gentle but insistent, his finger on my chin keeping me from looking away. "I want to hear your answer."

I forced my eyes to his. "Teach me, Luca."

A slow, seductive smile spread across his lips, and the pad of his forefinger dragged down from my chin to my throat, to my chest and between the valley of my cleavage.

He tugged my bra between the cups. "Take this off. I want to see you, mia bella." I reached with a hesitant hand behind me, still sitting beside him, but he stopped me. "Stand up, if you please. Make of it a dance, perhaps. You are so beautiful, Delilah. So sexy. Show me you know this."

I shook my head. I could barely whisper, but he heard it. "I'm not."

He looked almost sad. "Know it, in your heart. You are exquisite. Stand up." I stood up slowly, arms around myself, trying to cover my breasts and stomach. "Yes, very good. Now, put down your arms, just let me look. Feel your body. With your hands, feel yourself."

My breath shuddered, but I managed to force my arms down, and touched my hips above the fabric of my skirt. I ran my hands up my sides, touched the heavy cups of my bra and across the exposed cleavage, then down my arms. Luca seemed to enjoy this; the lust in his eyes gave me courage. I reached behind me for the zipper of my skirt, tugged it down, hooked my thumbs in the waistband, then hesitated.

"Yes, take it off. Show me more." Luca leaned back on his hands.

I could see the evidence of his arousal bulging against the zipper of his jeans. My blood boiled, both at my wanton behavior and at the thought of his manhood, hard for me.

I slipped the skirt over my hips, wiggled my backside and let my skirt pool on the floor, and then I was in only my bra and panties, and Luca clutched the bedspread in his fists, as if forcing himself to remain in place.

"*Mio dios. Così bella. Si guarda in modo morbido. Voglio toccarti.*"

"What? What did you just say?"

He laughed, a low rumble. His eyes never stopped roving my body. "I said, so beautiful. You look so soft, I want to touch you."

A burst of courage spurted through me: "So touch me."

He shook his head. "Not yet, but soon. First, show me more, mia bella. More."

My hands shook, and I looked away. I couldn't. Bare my body to a man?

"Please." It was a single soft word, said with a smile and a look of pure desire.

It was enough.

I reached behind me and unhooked the bra, a single eyelet at a time. I couldn't go any faster if I had wanted to. My hands were shaking like leaves in a long wind, and my heart was beating fit to burst from my chest. I was nearly hyperventilating. But I did it. I got the bra unhooked, and, with an effort of will, crossed my hands to opposite shoulders and brushed the straps off, let the bra fall to the ground.

My arms crossed in front automatically, and my spine hunched.

"Stand straight. Yes, like that. Very good. Now, lower your arms. Let me see your beautiful breasts."

I made my arms drop to my sides and stood straight. His breath was coming in deep pulls, his eyes half-lidded, his fists crumpling the bedspread.

"Now the rest."

This was even harder. Impossible. "I can't," I said.

"You can. You want to. You are lovely, and I want to see all of you. Show me."

I closed my eyes and took deep, calming breaths. I could do this. I *did* want to. He thought I was beautiful. Yes.

My hands ran down my sides, between my skin and the pink lace, pushed them down my thighs and I bent, breasts swaying, to step out of the panties. Eyes closed. Hands shaking in front of my sex. Chin trembling.

"Look at me, Delilah." Luca's voice was soft, tender, insistent.

I shook my head, rooted to the threadbare carpet.

I heard the springs release as Luca stood up, and my shaking grew worse. I reminded myself that I wanted this. Floorboards creaked, and heat assaulted my naked body as Luca drew near.

I gasped in shock as a finger traced the curve of my side and down my hip. I tilted my head back when I felt lips on my shoulder, lost my breath when they moved down to my chest, and then to the mound of one breast. Fingers trickled up my belly, dipped into my navel and continued upwards, a slow journey under my breasts and to my areolas, and then...

My knees buckled as he pinched my nipple, sending heat lightning zapping through my body, and his other hand was curving around my hip to cup one buttock, and all this while his lips were on my skin, touching my throat and my shoulder and my chest and cheek, and now my lips.

"Now look at me, Delilah. Please."

I looked. His eyes were on mine, patient and burning with desire. He put his hands on my shoulders and spun me in a half-turn, so I faced the bathroom door. I saw myself in the mirror, nude, pale as porcelain, voluptuous, with Luca standing shirtless in a pair of jeans behind me. His arms wrapped around me, across my belly, dark skin on white.

"Look how lovely you are," he said, his breath tickling my ear. "See? See how beautiful?"

"I see *you*," I said to Luca. "You're beautiful."

He stepped to the side, out of the mirror's frame, catching my hand in his. "Now look, it is only you. Now do you see your beauty?"

I shook my head. "I just see me." Again, the rush of daring; I turned away from the mirror and faced Luca. "Show me you think I'm beautiful. Continue my education."

He stepped toward me, closing the gap. "Help me with my pants," he said.

Oh, his education forced me so far out of my comfort zone; but then, just about everything did, didn't it?

I traced around the heavy, broad pectoral muscles, down between the canyons of his abdominal muscles, to his sides, and then the thick cords of his arms. He stood still and let me touch. Both hands now, all over his stomach. I kissed him, and now his lips on mine were slow and thorough, exploring my mouth with his, and I let my hands wander down to toy with the button of his jeans.

Was I going to do this?

Hell, yes.

The button slid out easily, and the zipper fell almost by itself, and then his pants spread apart, showing black cotton. A breath, and then I pushed the jeans down past his hips, and he stepped out of them, one foot on the loose fabric by his other foot, and then the opposite, and then he was in only a pair of tight black briefs, his erection outlined, the head nearly popping out the top.

My God, the man was beautiful.

"Almost there, *mia bella*. Now the underwear. Slowly."

Two hooked fingers curled inside the elastic band at his hipbones and tugged down. The tip of his penis caught the material, and I had to slide one finger around the band to free him. My finger brushed his manhood and I, absurdly, blushed. Down past his thighs, now, the briefs went, and my eyes were helpless to look away.

Comparisons are inevitable, at this point, aren't they?

Harry was my only point of reference, of course. According to Marge, he was...poorly endowed. Small. Of course, she may not have been telling the truth, or just trying to placate me in some odd way.

If Luca was any frame of comparison, Harry was barely there. Good gravy. A moment of objectivity. Harry was shorter by a matter of inches, and thinner by nearly as much.

I'd not really seen Harry erect, either before, during, or after sex. As I've said too many times, we never did anything in the light. Ridiculous as it may sound, I made it through nearly ten years of marriage without ever really seeing him naked, touching his sex, or much else for that matter.

I felt a moment of panic. If we, Luca and I, had sex...he was going to put that in there? He was huge. I'd be split in half.

My panic must have shown. "Please, don't worry. You will stretch. I will be slow, and you will tell me if it is uncomfortable. But that is not for now. Do not think of that." Luca pushed against me, his erection a hard but silken wedge between our bodies. "For now, it is only about one minute at a time, one moment by one moment. Now lie down, and let me touch you."

He pushed me to the bed and I lay down, scooting to the middle. Luca followed me, lying next to me, close enough to let his heat warm me. His lips touched mine, and I felt relief. I lost all my worries, all my fears, all my thoughts when he kissed me. I could do this, when he kissed me.

Maybe he knew this, and pulled away to make me feel my fear and face it. He kissed me on the jaw, then my throat underneath my chin, and then the hollow at the base of my neck. My fingers found the back of his head and rested there. He moved lower, and lower, and...oh...god...

His mouth was on my nipple, teeth grazing, lips pinching. Pure delight. There was never, in all my life, anything so wonderful as Luca's mouth on my breast at that moment, his lips grazing the full curves, tongue teasing, flicking, circling. Wet heat bloomed between my thighs, in the folds of my pussy. His hand found my other nipple, and then, holy heaven and good gravy, he put his fingers to my sex, pressed his palm to my mound and dipped a single finger inside me.

This was in no way like touching myself. He was all over me, kissing my breasts, fingering my nipple, touching my pussy. All I could do was arch my back and remember to breathe.

The finger inside me moved, then, a slow swipe, an exploratory delving into my depths, sweeping the walls and then back out. Oh, oh god, he found my clit, then, sweet Jesus...lightning blasted through me when he circled the aching nub with two fingers.

"You are so tight, *mia bella*. So wet." He spoke with his mouth still at my nipple. "I wonder… yes…I wonder how you *taste*."

"What? No, you can't…"

He did.

His body moved down and his hands pushed my resisting knees apart, and his mouth kissed a hot line up my thigh, higher and higher, to the patch of trimmed curls.

I've always kept myself trimmed down there, just because that's how I like it.

I tried to squeeze my knees together, mortified, embarrassed, shocked that he would put his mouth there, but he only kissed more ardently, tonguing my opposite thigh, and then the mound of my pubis and—yes, yes, sweet ecstasy—his tongue found my entrance, drove in and up, pulled back and licked again. He kissed the lips of my pussy, then pushed his tongue back in, and I was a bridge, spine arching at every touch of his tongue.

He'd just gotten started, it seemed. He flicked the wet button of my clit, then, and I jerked, gasping, but he didn't relent, or stop, only licked again, and now his fingers were inside me even as his tongue began to find a rhythm, around and around and around, then up and up and up.

I wasn't sure what he did next, but something exploded deep inside me. His middle and ring finger touched a spot on the inside, high up, and I came apart. His tongue lapped against my clit and his fingers rubbed that spot and I was a gyrating, undulating bundle of ecstatic nerve endings, whimpering, bucking, but he stayed with me and kept going, kept going...

The world ended, for a moment, and I may have screamed.

Luca's weight was next to me again, and when I could move, I rolled into him and met his eyes. "Oh...my...God. How did you do that?"

"You liked it?" I could only nod, grinning shyly against his shoulder. "Good. I will do it again, if you wish, later." He kissed me, and I tasted my own musk on his tongue.

I found myself glancing down at his erection... at his cock. The word rolled through my head, and I said it mentally, trying it. Cock. I want to touch him, I thought. I want to touch his cock.

"Go ahead," he said, and I realized I'd spoken aloud.

I didn't giggle. Really.

Okay, fine, I did, just a little.

I put my hand on his chest and ran it south to his belly, and then my palm was gliding along his cock. It was...so many contradicting sensations. Hard but soft at the same time. Hard as steel, but a little springy under my fingers, and silky smooth, warm. Long, and thick. I wrapped a fist around him, and my fingers barely met. His eyes shuddered and squeezed closed, and I realized then the effect I was having on him. He liked this. He enjoyed my touch.

I slipped my hand down his length, then put my other hand around him, fist above fist, and then a single drop of clear liquid seeped out the hole at the top, the name of which I couldn't remember at the time and it doesn't matter now, as I write this. I moved my hands together up his length and then back down, mimicking the action of sex, squeezing gently.

His testicles were tight against him, and I touched them too, cupped them in my palm, amazed at how much heavier they were than I expected. I returned my hands to his cock, and let them simply touch and explore.

I was amazed at myself, at my calm as I wrapped my fingers around the cock of a man I'd just met.

His hands caught mine and he pushed them away. "Enough, for now. If you continue, this will be over before it has begun."

I knew, clinically speaking what would happen. I'd never seen it happen, though. Harry always came inside me. I wanted to see it happen. I wanted to make it happen.

"I want to, though. I mean, I want to make you...you know. Like you did for me."

Luca smiled and cupped my breast, leaned over me and kissed me. "Oh, you will. And later, you can do what you want to me. For now, though, I want to be here," he said as he touched two fingers to my pussy.

Logic pushed through me. "I'm on the pill," I told him.

There were other considerations I knew I should ask about, but his mouth found my nipple again, and he was leaning above me, touching me with his fingers, fluttering inside me.

"That is good. And I am clean, tested regularly, nothing to worry about," Luca said, kneeling between my thighs. "Now, look at me, Delilah."

I ran my hands up his sides, rested them on his back, looking up at him.

"Are you sure? You want this? I will stop. Now, or during, just tell me."

I closed my eyes and breathed deep, searched myself for doubts, and found only nerves, but no fear, no doubts. "Just…be gentle."

He moved closer, and then there was a presence, a hard, moist tip pushing into me, his eyes on mine, watching for my reaction. I flattened my palms on his back and held my breath as he slid in. He was slow, so, so slow. An inch, and then a pause, one hand supporting his weight, the other toying with my breast and my nipple.

Another thrust, a little deeper, and I felt my wetness slicking him, felt my muscles burning pleasantly as he stretched me to accommodate, and oh god, oh god, it never felt like this before. Not with such desire, such appreciation in Luca's eyes, his hands on me, exploring my skin, his body moving him deeper into me.

He made an "mmmmm" noise in the back of his throat and plunged all the way in, our hips bumping, and then I felt the fluttering pressure low in my belly. He held there, and now I was so wet, so wet, so full of him, past full, and he slid out so all that remained inside was the very tip. This time he slid in to the hilt in one thrust, and I gasped, mouth wide, head arched back, and my fingers scrabbled at his back.

The next thrust was smoother, out and back in, his full length drawing out and spearing in and the heat was spreading, the pressure burgeoning. Again, and again, and now my legs were around his buttocks and pulling him against me, because yes I loved this, wanted it so much, it felt so good.

A rhythm was begun, now, faster and faster, and I was wavering on the edge of detonation, and then...

He rolled, and I was above him. "You do it, now. Take the pleasure for yourself, at your pace." Luca was staring up at me, hands at my waist.

This was new. He was even deeper inside me, like this. The angle of our bodies stretched his cock away from his body, and forced it higher within me. I tried an experimental roll of my hips...

This was nice. Oh yes...A girl could get used to this. His hands held my waist and lifted me up, let me fall down and then lifted again. He wasn't controlling or guiding the pace, only showing me, and I didn't mind, his hands around my waist felt natural and perfect. My weight was on my knees and shins, and I lifted up, feeling his slick length drag out of me, igniting every nerve ending and eliciting a gasp, and then I sank back down, *God*, so deep and there was no stopping me now from the sink-and-rise rhythm of his body inside mine.

He was grunting and whispering my name and chanting something in Italian, sounding like a song—it could have been *sì, tutto bene* but I'm not sure—and he helped me lift and fall, pulling me down onto him, harder and harder now and the storm of heat and lightning and fire in my belly and my veins was raging out of control. My hands were flat on his belly, my spine straight and then bending and straightening as I rode him closer and closer to climax.

No, this was nothing at all like what I did to myself in the Chicago hotel room; the two sensations were almost unrelated. This was raw intensity, pleasure beyond the capacity of words to convey.

My hips were driving like a madwoman's, now, and Luca was exhorting me onwards, his head thrown back and his hips punching up into mine, his eyes closed and his breath ragged and his lovely, perfect masculine body sheened in sweat.

Oh, Lord, was he right. Whatever I'd done before bore no resemblance to this. *This* was sex. *This* was making love. I knew I'd just met Luca, but I felt a frightening balloon of emotion expanding in my chest, all centered around Luca and this lesson in sensate delight. I didn't know what it was or what it meant, and I didn't care.

All thoughts were blown away, then, all knowledge of past or present or future. All was pleasure, so pure and raw and intense that it simply defies my control of words to capture.

I collapsed on him, our hips still rolling into each other with the fury of clashing storms, my arms curled under his head and clutching him with all the power of my locked and spasming muscles.

I felt him come, an instant before I did. He said my name and exploded within me, releasing a jet of wet heat against my farthest inner walls, "De-LI-lah," he said with a thrust on the middle syllable, his hips driving into me with slow, ravaging power. Feeling him come, I couldn't remain on this side of sanity. I dissolved on top of him, fell into trembling, shuddering, gasping tremors as every cell in my body came alive as never before.

Luca was holding tight to me, fingers digging into my sides, breathing as if he'd run a marathon. I was limp, completely exhausted, all frayed, sated nerve endings. I was a puddle on top of him, and I couldn't have moved if I wanted. He turned with me so we were on our sides, his shaft still buried inside me.

"That..." I started, but words failed me. "That was so..."

"Amazing," Luca breathed. "So, so amazing."

I looked at him, met his burning brown eyes. "I didn't know...I didn't know it could be like that."

"Nor did I, and I am not new at this as you are."

"That was good for you too?" I asked.

Luca laughed, a full belly laugh of amazement. "Delilah...it was more than amazing. It was...I do not know all the words at this moment...it was powerful."

I didn't know what to say in response, so I didn't say anything, just nestled closer into his arms and tried to contain the baffling welter of emotions and sensations inside me.

Silence blossomed between us, comfortable and easy, the afterglow settling upon us like a heated blanket. I was just beginning to drowse into slumber when Luca spoke again.

"So, are you coming home with me tomorrow?"

My heart froze. Home?

"Come home with you?" My voice was tight and tense.

Luca caught it and spoke hesitantly. "Yes, home. To my parents' house for my holiday. I asked you to travel to Firenze with me."

"I thought you meant, I don't know...that you'd take me to a hotel or something."

Luca brushed hair from my forehead. "Well, I could, but that is not what I was meaning. My parents' home, it is big enough for you to have a room as well. Cheaper than a hotel, no? And more comfortable." He lifted up on an elbow. "I only meant it as a convenience, not—it does not mean what I think you are fearing. I mean, it could, because I have a great affection for you, though we are only friends recently."

Luca was nervous. His English, normally fluent, if accented and sometimes strangely structured, was growing harder to follow.

"Luca, I—"

What did I want? Maybe he just meant it as a kindness, or as he said, a convenience. But what if he wanted more than I could give? To say I'd enjoyed having sex with him would be an understatement. I wanted it again, and again. I felt insatiable, as if I could have him time and again and never be fully sated.

But did that mean I wanted to meet his parents? Did that hold the same import here as it did in America? I didn't know.

He sensed my rush of confusion. "You do not need to answer now. Maybe just sleep and we can talk more when the morning has come."

I nodded and let myself drift, thoughts spinning in wild circles. Luca fell asleep, and so did I, but I woke again in the wee, cold hours of the morning, my mind a jumble of emotions.

I left the bed, put Luca's T-shirt on and dug my netbook out of my bag, opened it to my diary and started writing. I can't believe how much I've written, and as I read it, I can't believe the things I've written. I don't know what to think, what to want. My heart is still a mess over the end of my eight-year marriage, and Harry's infidelity and my sudden status as a single woman alone in the world. And now there's Luca, sleeping in my bed, broad back bare to the dim night, muscles shifting and expanding as he breathes.

I can't deny the pang of affection that stabs my heart as I sit in the corner and write this, watching him sleep. What does that mean? Do I want to find out?

I don't know.

Part of me wants to run, to pack my things and sneak out of Rome...Roma...and find the first bus or train or taxi to somewhere else, somewhere far away from the dangerous slew of emotions the huge, gorgeous man in my bed has spawned.

Run. Run. Run.

The word hammers to the rhythm of my terrified heartbeat. It was supposed to be just sex, just a lesson in the arts of love. But…oh shit. The arts of love. I'd taken that to mean the arts of making love. What if he meant something else? We just met, a few hours ago. How could he mean that? And wasn't the woman supposed to be the one to attach emotions to a physical thing?

I'm going in circles, but I can't deny the urge to flee.

It's three in the morning, and I've just had sex with a stranger, and I don't know what I'm feeling, because he's not a stranger. I know him. But I don't, and I can't, and…

Run. Run. Run.

I wonder if I can find a bus to Venice at this hour?

Delilah's Diary 2: La Vita Sexy

June 12

THE AIR WAS SHARP AND COLD, the night dark around me, the city silent. I dragged my suitcase behind me, the tiny wheels bumping on the cobblestones, tipping the suitcase every other step.

I was running like a coward. Running from Luca, running from my feelings and my fears and from myself. But mainly from Luca. He was too much, too sexy, too amazing.

I had no idea where I was going, or what my plan was, other than to just go.

Run. Run. Run.

Every step made my heart hurt, made me feel more and more like a coward, a silly girl. But I couldn't make myself turn around and go back to him. He was sleeping so peacefully, and if I came back in, he'd hear me and wake up and want to know where I had gone, and I didn't know how to explain what was happening in my head, my heart.

A footstep echoed behind me, a shuffle and a scrape. Whispers in Italian, low male laughter. More than one voice. I tried to ignore them, quickened my pace along the street. I didn't even know the name of the street I was on, or if buses ran at this time of night, or morning, or whatever three a.m. was.

The laughter and the footsteps were closer, and I desperately wanted to turn and look to see who was following me. I didn't. I kept walking. Kept walking. Ignored the laughter, ignored the steps only a few feet behind me now.

Shit. This was stupid. I should have stayed. I could have told Luca I didn't want to go home with him. He would have understood. I could have gone to Firenze with him and stayed somewhere alone, and spent time with him, in a less frightening situation.

"Hey, *bella*. Where you goin'?" A foot kicked my suitcase aside, and I had to stop to right it.

Three young men, dark hair, scruffy not-quite-beards, acne, skinny jeans, and evil, leering grins. One of them kicked my suitcase again, this time knocking it from my grasp. I left it where it lay and stood my ground in front of them. The one who'd kicked my suitcase slipped away from his friends and squatted by my suitcase. He opened it, pulled clothes out of it, and tossed them to the ground. He plucked a thong and held it up, sniffed it.

"You wearin' one of these?" He licked his lips as he dangled the thong from a finger. "I think you are. You show me, *sì*?"

He flicked a glance at his two friends and they moved apart, trying to flank me. I backed up, trying to keep all three in view. The one with my panties rose lithely to his feet and stalked toward me. His eyes roved over my body; I had slipped on a pair of shorts and a T-shirt, and the shorts were suddenly much shorter than I'd remembered.

The three closed in around me, now darting to tighten the noose. I felt hands clutch my arms from behind, hard, cruel fingers holding me tight. Other hands plucked at my shirt, lifting it...

Before I could scream, I heard a foot scrape, then a rustling of clothes, and then Luca was there, jerking the one holding my thong off his feet, bashing him in the face with a quick, merciless fist. I was released and I scrambled backward, thumping into a wall. Luca was a whirlwind, dodging fists and ducking, slamming his own return blows, all of this silent, only the sounds of fists meeting flesh and grunts.

Then the hoodlums were running away, and Luca dragged a wrist across his bleeding nose. He turned to face me, his eyes a blaze of confusion, pain, and anger.

"What in hell were you thinking?" He stomped toward me, fists balled, shoulders tensed, his gait aggressive.

I cringed instinctively, and he immediately softened.

"I am sorry, I am not angry at you, only...confused." He stopped within arm's reach of me, but didn't touch me. "Are you okay? Did they hurt you? Touch you?"

I shook my head. "I'm okay. They didn't do anything. But...if you hadn't come when you did..."

The reality of what had almost happened hit me then, and I trembled, swayed, and fell. Luca caught me and sank to the ground with me in his arms.

"Why did you leave?" His voice was soft, his eyes betraying genuine worry and hurt.

I'd hurt him by sneaking out. My gut clenched, and my heart was stabbed with a pang of guilt.

"I...I don't know. I was afraid. I'm sorry, Luca. It wasn't you, or...not because—" I wasn't making sense. I took a breath and started over. "Everything just overwhelmed me, all of a sudden."

Luca helped me stand up and gathered my clothes into my suitcase. He took my suitcase in one hand, carrying it rather than rolling it, and held out his other hand for me. He had blood smeared on his wrist and dripping from his nose. I took his hand. We walked in silence back to the hotel room.

When we were back inside, I pushed Luca down into a chair and grabbed a towel from the bathroom to hold against his nose.

"I'm sorry, Luca. I shouldn't have run." I kept my eyes on his as I spoke, forcing myself to face up to what I saw in them. "It was all so...intense, and scary. I don't...I didn't...god, I'm not making any sense. It wasn't you..."

"You are saying the same things, but you are not saying why it is you did leave." Luca held my wrist as I dabbed at his nose. "You are afraid of feelings, I think. You see that I am feeling things for you, and this frightens you."

I nodded. "I'm not ready to feel things. I don't know where I'm going, or what I'm doing, or who I am. I'm just...still figuring it all out."

His nose had stopped bleeding, and he washed his hands and face in the bathroom sink. He flexed his fists, and I realized he'd split his knuckles open. I moved to dab at them as well, but he waved me off.

"Is nothing, please, not to worry." He nudged me toward the bed and sat down on the edge next to me. "You are thinking too hard, worrying too much. You are on holiday; you must only have fun and relax. Do not worry about me, or what I do feel or don't feel. If you don't want to come with me to Firenze, then don't. If you don't want to stay in my parents' house, then don't. I will understand, any choice you are making."

I yawned and stretched. Luca pushed me down and tugged my shoes off. "You must sleep. You have had a difficult day, and now a difficult night. Sleep, rest. I will be here when you wake up, and you will tell me what you wish to do. For now, no worries. You are safe."

I was still wearing the tight shorts and the T-shirt, and I knew myself well enough to know I'd never sleep with them on. I glanced at Luca, then down at my shorts. It was ridiculous, since I'd already stripped for him, and done…god…such incredible things with him, but the idea of taking off my shorts in front of him brought all my fears and insecurities rushing back through me. This time, though, it was the innocent intimacy of getting ready to sleep that had my heart pounding. I'd never slept next to another man before. Never gotten ready for bed with another man before.

New Delilah, new experiences. I repeated the phrase to myself. New me, new choices. No holding back.

I took a deep breath and stood up, unbuttoned my shorts and pushed them off, acting as casual as I could despite my thundering heart and trembling knees. Luca was watching me, and I could feel the desire in his gaze, could feel it prickling my skin. He didn't move to touch me, and I was alternately grateful and disappointed.

I pulled my arms out of the sleeves, unhooked my bra, and set it aside. As I slipped my arms back through, Luca chuckled.

"I never get tired of watching that," he said. "Is always funny, for some reason. You girls can change clothes in the middle of a crowd without revealing a single inch of skin."

I shrugged. "It's one of those things you just learn as a girl."

I brushed my teeth and then went back to the bed. Luca was still sitting there, watching me, waiting. Standing near the bed, I had to summon my courage once more. Oddly, climbing in bed to sleep was as nerve-wracking as stripping for him in preparation to have sex. I felt a rush of excitement at the memory of what we'd done together just a few hours before. What I wanted to do again. Right then.

A tiny part of my brain told me I should still be upset over what had almost happened, but honestly, Luca coming to the rescue like he had only turned me on. He had appeared out of nowhere, a knight to my fair maiden. He'd bled for me. That sent a thrill of heat shuddering through me, settling between my thighs.

I wanted him.

An errant thought passed through my head: Was this a one-night stand? If I slept with him again, now, or tomorrow, and the next day, did that change it into something else? I wasn't sure if I liked the idea of a one-night stand. I had committed myself to trying new things, to moving past the long-ingrained religious mores and taboos I'd grown up with. But did that mean I had to abandon all of my principles? Where did I draw the line? I'd already slept with Luca and couldn't deny how earth-shattering it had been. I couldn't deny how badly I wanted to experience that with him, again and again.

"You are thinking very hard, aren't you, *mia bella* Delilah?" Luca stood up and wrapped his arms around my waist. "Tell me, if you will, what it is you are thinking about."

I thunked my forehead against his chest, spoke muffled words into his shirt. "About you. What we did together, and how much I liked it. About how I...how I want to do it again." I looked up at him, forced my eyes to lock with his. "But I'm also wondering about what it means."

He tilted his head to the side. "What it means? I do not understand this. What should it mean? Two adults can do this together without it having a deep meaning, can they not?"

"Well, that's exactly what I'm wondering about. Yes, they can. And it happens all the time, just…just not to me. And I was raised…differently. I was raised to believe sex should only happen in the context of marriage. That sex outside marriage was a sin. When everything with my ex-husband happened, it threw into question everything I believed. I…resolved to start over. Do things I'd never considered doing before. Experience life, you know? And then I met you, and I wanted to do… what we did. And I want to again, but I keep…I don't know…fighting with myself over whether I think it's wrong or not. My upbringing tells me it is, and my body tells me it's not, and my mind and heart don't know what to think."

Luca's brows furrowed as he absorbed what I'd said. "That is very complicated."

I laughed, a bit mirthlessly. "Yeah, that's me. Complicated. Sorry."

He chuckled. "No, I do not mean to say you are complicated, just all that you are thinking. I did not imagine it would be so deep a subject when I asked."

"Oh, Luca. When you hooked up with me, you got a whole lot more than you'd probably imagined, on a lot of levels." I leaned into him, flattening my palms against his shoulders. I was worried he was about to leave, and wanted to get as much contact with him as I could before he was gone.

"Are you wishing things were simpler with me?" I asked. "I know I'm complicated, and I'm sorry. I wish I could simplify things, but…I'm just a mess right now, I guess."

Luca looked down at me in puzzlement. "You should not apologize for who you are. No, Delilah. I do not wish you were less complicated. You are who you are, and I knew you were not a simple person from the first moment we met. I like this about you. I am not afraid of the challenge of understanding you."

That took a moment for me to work out in my head. "I'm a challenge to you?"

Luca laughed and rolled his eyes at me. "Yes, you are. This is not meant to be an insult, so please, do not be so offended. You cannot apologize for not being simpler, and then be insulted when I say understanding you for your complexness is a challenge. It is illogical."

I laughed and pushed him playfully. "Hasn't anyone ever told you women are illogical?"

"Well, yes, but—"

"Relax. I wasn't offended. If you're up to the challenge that is Delilah Flores, then that's your choice. I just want you to understand what you're getting into."

"Oh, I know very well what I am getting into," Luca said, his voice husky.

The teasing banter had shifted suddenly. Now the sparks of humor were turning into sparks of heat. I realized, in the back of my head, that we'd agreed, in a sideways kind of way, to an ongoing relationship of some kind. I pushed away the thought before I could freak myself out.

I focused instead on the way Luca's hands were inching down from my back to the hem of my shirt, and the heat of his palms on my skin, and the dampness spreading between my thighs at his touch.

"You are supposed to be sleeping," Luca said.

"I'm not tired, suddenly," I said.

He was stroking my back underneath my shirt, but in a soothing way rather than a sensual way. His eyes were full of desire, and I could feel his erection growing between us, but he was holding back. He didn't want to push me, I realized.

I would have to show him what I wanted.

I stepped back away from him and pulled my shirt off, then stripped my panties away. He licked his lips and reached for me. I pushed his hands down, an idea in my head that I intended to follow through with before I lost my nerve.

I peeled his T-shirt over his head, pushed his jeans off, and then nudged him onto the bed. He lay down, his underwear tented by his burgeoning erection. I climbed onto the bed and leaned over him, planted a kiss on his chest, between his pectoral muscles, and then again on his belly. He tucked a pillow under his head and watched me with burning eyes. I met his gaze and slipped my fingers under the elastic of his underwear, pulling them down past his hips and off.

I ran my palms over his body, across his broad chest and washboard stomach, down his thighs and back up, finally coming to rest on his cock. He twitched, and caught my hands.

"Delilah—"

"I want to. I want to touch you." I pulled my hands free and grasped his shaft in both hands. I lowered my mouth to him, kissed his hip. "I want to taste you."

Luca lifted up on an elbow. "Delilah, you do not have to...please, just let me make love to you."

I looked at him across the expanse of his body, wondering why he was hung up on this. Maybe he didn't believe that I wanted to. I slipped my fists up and down his length, caressed his sack in one hand, then extended a hesitant tongue and touched it to his cock, just beneath the head.

He tasted like skin, and male musk, and faintly of me.

"I want to. I've never done this before, and I want to. I wouldn't do it if I didn't."

He laid back down, then, a smile curving his mouth.

"Do you want me to?" I asked. "Do you like it?"

He laughed, a low rumble in his chest. "Of course. Do not let any man tell you he doesn't like it. So yes, I do want it, but I also don't want you to think you have to, only because I did it to you."

I shrugged, and licked him again, then said, "It's certainly not that. I really, *really* liked it when you did that, and I hope you'll do it again, but that's not why. I want to know how you taste. I want to…just because I do. Now shut up."

He laughed again. "As you wish, *mia bella*."

I licked the tip, swiping my tongue over the soft, salty head. His breath caught, and his belly sucked in. "Just…tell me if I'm doing it wrong, okay?"

Luca laughed, tangling his fingers in my hair. "Only do not bite me, is all I ask. Anything else you could do will be right. There is no right way or wrong way."

I took a deep breath, held it, and then lowered my mouth to him. My heart was pounding in my chest. I was filled with excitement, desire, and a little twinge of guilt at what I was about to do.

I touched my lips to the head of his cock, kissing him, and then opened my jaw and took him into my mouth, just an inch or two at first. He was thick, hard but soft and springy at the same time. He was big enough that I had to stretch my jaw and my lips to take all of him. A bit more, then, deeper into my mouth. I wrapped my fingers around his base, near the close-trimmed curls of hair, moving lightly, letting my fingers barely brush him.

"Oh, *mio dio*," he gasped, arching his back.

He liked it, then. I must have been doing something right. I took more of him into my mouth, and then he was at the back of my throat and I was struggling not to gag. I backed off a bit, moving my hand more vigorously now, and I felt him quivering, straining to hold still. I widened my throat muscles and went deeper again, and this time ignored the gag reflex.

Luca gasped, cursing in Italian, tightening his fingers on my hair. He liked it deep, then. I didn't mind, now that I knew what to expect. I lifted my head so he was almost free of my lips, and then bobbed back down, slowly, still pumping at his base. He scrabbled at the bed with his heels, clutched the sheet with his fists, eyes closed, head tipped back. Every muscle in his body was tensed, and his spine was bowing upward, as if straining to go deeper. So I took him deeper, until I couldn't anymore, and then backed away, deeper, back away...

He was groaning now, both hands in my short red hair, his hips moving of their own accord, fluttering up and down. I moved my mouth on him in the rhythm of his hips' rise and fall, moving down on him as he rose up. I didn't take him so deep I had to fight the gag reflex, but close.

"*Sto per...*" he said, gasping. "I am...*dio*..."

He was mixing English and Italian, not making complete sentences in either language. I loved the effect I was having on him. He was clearly lost in the throes of extreme pleasure, and even if I didn't find any physical pleasure in doing this to him, I found myself enjoying doing it to him, giving him such extreme pleasure.

His fingers tightened in my hair until my scalp tingled, and then he gasped, saying something in Italian that I didn't quite catch. I felt his balls contract in my palm. He was coming, I realized. That's what he had been trying to say, warning me. I felt a burst of fear, wondering how it would taste, how it would feel, and what was I supposed to do with it, with his come? Did I spit it out? Swallow it?

I didn't have time to think then. He jerked his hips and I took him deep, sucked until my cheeks hollowed, and when I did he grunted loudly, something like *sì*, but I wasn't sure, and it didn't matter because I felt something thick, hot, and salty hit my tongue, and then another spasm and another shot of his come splashed against my throat and ran down. I swallowed, realizing I didn't have much choice, because he was still coming, another gush of tangy, thick heat in my mouth.

He gasped again, raggedly, and I slipped him out of my mouth, but continued to move my hands on him until he captured my wrists in his hands and pulled me up against his chest. I wiped my lips on my wrist, still tasting his come, still feeling his cock stretching my lips and jaw.

I wasn't sure what I thought of having given my first blow job. I tried to analyze my feelings. It wasn't bad, I didn't dislike it. He was gasping and trembling still, clutching me against him as if he never wanted to let go. I liked that part. I liked what it did to him. I didn't like gagging, but if I didn't take him so deep next time that wouldn't happen. The rest was…fun. His come didn't taste bad at all. I loved his cock, loved feeling it, holding it, tasting it.

"*Mio dio*, Delilah," Luca whispered into my hair. "That was…*sorprendente*…amazing."

I nuzzled his shoulder, pleased and embarrassed. "You liked it?" I ran my hands on his chest and belly. "I mean…I did okay, for my first time?"

Luca laughed, incredulous. "Okay? *Dio*, Delilah. I've never…never was it so good. You have never done that before? I am not so sure I believe you. What did you think?"

I shrugged, uncomfortable talking about it. "It was…fun, for the most part. I liked how much you liked it."

"But?"

"I'm not sure I like gagging on you, though."

Luca laughed, gently. "Well, that is…how do I say it with tact? You do not have to allow that to happen. Most women…I know, do not like that, either. It is a thing that they think men like, so some will do it, to please the man, or to impress, perhaps?

But I think the men who like to see a woman feel gagged in that action, it is only because they find some...perverse pleasure in the...I cannot think of the word. To make feel less? To downgrade?"

"Degrade?"

"Yes, that is it, thank you. Those men like to degrade the woman, to feel themselves more powerful." Luca nudged my face so I was looking at him; his eyes were gentle and affectionate, frighteningly so. "Delilah, you must please listen closely. I do not like that. To degrade you, it is...not my wish. I want you to feel good for yourself. To have esteem about your mind and your body and your heart, all of you. I do not wish that kind of pretended, negative power over you."

He kissed me, put a finger over my lips to forestall anything I might say.

"To pleasure me like that...with your mouth, it feels good for me, yes? But not so good as being with you, in you. If you wish to do that, of your own choice, then I will like it. But do not think you must, or should, or need to, only to please me." He brushed his fingers through my hair, smiling at me. "You understand?"

I nodded.

"Now...let me see what I can do to make you feel as I do," Luca said, smiling at me.

He kissed my throat, and then my shoulder, and then between my breasts. I felt his palms skim my skin, slide past my face and to my nipples. I felt a quiver hit my belly, a rush of pure anticipation. He'd done this once before, so I knew what he was going to do and how it would feel, and good gravy, did I want it. I wanted his tongue on me, his fingers in me, right then. But, of course, he made me wait. I suppose that's a good thing, since it enhanced the anticipation. He traveled down my body with his lips at a leisurely pace, slipping lower and lower, lips touching the curves of my breasts, the padded bone of my ribs, the ivory drum of my belly. I trembled all over, tangled my fingers in his hair, my breath coming faster and faster as he moved closer to my wet, aching sex. He was so close, I wanted to push his face into me, but I didn't. I forced my hands to rest lightly in his inky hair and wait for him to find my folds at his own pace.

Time seemed to stop as he grew nearer to my pussy, kissing the round muscle of my thighs, outside first, then the inside. I ached, feeling a whelming pressure in the depths of my womanhood. One of his hands found my breast, cupped and palmed and held it, then rolled a taut nipple between gentle, calloused fingers. I gasped, and then moaned as he lapped at my labia, slow upward strokes at first, testing my folds, tasting them.

"Yes, Luca, more..." I said, the words escaping from me.

He complied, drove his tongue into me, split my nether lips apart to taste my juices. His unoccupied hand trailed across my belly, past his chin, and two fingers slipped into my pussy, curled up to stroke the sensitive patch of rough skin. I whimpered and arched my back. He rolled his tongue around my clit, pinching my nipple and circling my G-spot all in the same motion, same rhythm. Faster now, bringing my hips to a bucking frenzy and my breathing to ragged gasps...and then he slowed, almost to a stop.

I did pull his face against me then, and he resumed a quick lapping, but matched it with a slow circling of his fingers inside me while flicking my nipple gently. I couldn't think of much, but I did have a moment of respect for his ability to multi-task.

Now the whelming pressure in my loins spread, turned molten and then fiery. The trembling in my legs became shaking, the quivering in my belly became a desperate rolling of my hips into his mouth.

All at once, everything exploded. I saw stars flash across my eyes and every muscle in my body turned liquid, jellified by electric orgasm. Luca's breath sucked in against my folds, a blast of cold air, and then he breathed out, a gout of hot air, and then the electricity became unbearable, overwhelming. My trembling and shaking became spastic and my moans shrieks of pleasure as he licked and licked, stroked and stroked.

And then I passed the point of frenzy and fell into helplessness, my legs going limp, my hands heavy on his shoulders, and I felt a lazy thought float through me: *I wonder if his jaw and tongue get tired?*

I drew him up to me, clutching his head by the jaw and ears, clumsy and floppy, seeing flashes in front of my eyes, aftershocks shuddering my entire lower half. I clung to him, barely able to breathe.

Just when I was beginning to catch my breath and cease trembling, I felt something nudge my hip. I knew what it was, rolled to my side and smiled at Luca as I wrapped my fingers around his thick, rigid, ready cock. It wasn't so limp, suddenly.

Luca leaned over me, touched his lips to mine, a hesitant, questing brush. I lifted up to deepen the kiss, pulled him over on top of me. My hands rested on his back as we kissed, in no hurry for this moment, simply reveling in the exploration of mouths. I felt his fingers hunt for my opening, and then his soft yet firm tip pierced me, slid deep into my pussy and fluttered with our hips flush.

He didn't pull out and thrust yet but stayed deep, light, delicate flits, just enough to send thrills up my spine. I pulled my knees up to allow him deeper, rocked my buttocks to get a good thrust out of him, growing impatient now. I wanted the motion, wanted the glide in and slip out, the build of pressure and spread of fire.

Luca wrapped his arms underneath my knees and lifted my legs up and straightened his torso. Kneeling over me now, he shifted forward, rested my heels on his shoulders, and then thrust.

I went cross-eyed with ecstasy. He was deeper than I thought possible this way, and then he withdrew so only the broad tip of his cock was inside. He pulsed there, at my entrance, clutching my ass to hold me aloft.

He drove hard, slashing into my wet pink folds. I arched my back, grasped at the sheet, and breathed a whimper. Out again, a brief ache of absence, and then he was gliding in and back out, and again, smooth, slow strokes. No rhythm yet, just Luca's throbbing manhood plunging in to stutter against my farthest inner wall, stuttering, slipping, sliding, Luca's gorgeous features limned with sweat and moonlight, his marvelously muscled body moving, contorting, shifting.

"God, yes, Luca," I breathed. "More. Harder."

"Harder?" Luca grinned and clutched my thighs against his chest. "This I can do...*mia bella* Delilah."

Harder he went, moving into me with primal rhythm, resting his cheek against my ankle, kissing my leg, thrusting hard and hard and hard, and now...oh, god...

I was splintered by lightning in my belly, broken apart by a flood of release. I came again, a coiling detonation flinging me into the furthest fires of passion. And still he moved, lost within me now, delving deep and drawing nearly out, eyes closed, mouth curled in feral grin, midnight locks of hair drifting across his brow, olive skin sheened with sweat.

He grunted, a low growl in the bottom of his throat, adjusted his grip on my legs and thrust harder, faster, deeper. I was drowning in climax, rolling, rollicking, frenzied and wild, shrieking as he plunged into me.

This was better than the last one, which had been better than the one before…if this continued, I couldn't fathom what they would feel like in a day, a week.

He came, then, and oh, my god, he came hard. He crashed into me, hot wet seed flooding through me, spurting against my walls with every thrust, his face thrown back to the ceiling and locked in a rictus of pleasure as he plunged into me. Our bodies clashed together, came together. At length, Luca went still, pulled out and collapsed next to me, cradling my head on his chest and curling an arm around me.

I slept then, held close, feeling safe and protected.

When I woke, the sun was shining high through the window and Luca was in the shower. I slid up in bed, feeling sore in a pleasant way, sated and yet hungry. My netbook was in my bag next to the bed, and I opened it to write this entry. Luca emerged from the shower about a thousand words ago, kissed me, caressed me, distracted me, and then left to bring back breakfast and let me write. I'm done now, I think, and ready for a shower.

The question is answered, in my mind.

I'm going to Firenze with Luca. I don't know if I'll stay at his parents' house or not, but I'll decide that when we get there.

June 13

Luca drove a pretty little red Citroën DS4. I showed a hint of interest in how pretty the little car was, and like men the world over, Luca was off and running, a flood of half-English, half-Italian exuberance over its performance specs and features and whatnot. What I took away from his impromptu lecture was, primarily, its name, that it was fast, and it was pretty. Most little cars like that get called "cute," but somehow Luca's car didn't seem cute to me. It was pretty, like a sports car almost.

We left Rome around eleven in the morning after a leisurely breakfast in the hotel room.

"How long will it take to get to Florence?" I asked.

"Oh, it is a sort of long drive," Luca said. "Perhaps three hours? If we go direct and without stopping, possible less. But I think maybe we will stop some of the way there and have a lunch."

I laughed. "You call three hours a long drive?"

Luca smiled at me. "It is kind of long. Remember, I drive all over Italia selling the wines, so I am in the car all the time. For me, it is not so long. For someone who only lives in one city and does not often leave, yes, it would be trip for a whole day."

"Three hours is nothing," I said. "My ex-husband's family lives in Montana, and we drive—used to drive, I mean...from Illinois to Missoula for the holidays. Now, *that's* a long drive."

"These places, they are a long way apart?" Luca asked.

"It's a full twenty-four hours of driving. We live—lived, I mean—near Peoria, which is central Illinois, and his folks lived in Missoula, which is near the far western border of Montana. It's, like... fifteen hundred miles? A little more?"

"And how often did you do this holiday?"

"Oh, at least once a year. We'd drive up for Thanksgiving and they'd come down for Christmas. Sometimes we'd switch."

Luca glanced at me, one hand resting on the gear shifter. "Do you miss him? Tell me truly."

I stared out the window and the lush scenery passing by, thinking. "I've tried not to think about it. I guess I do, in a way. I mean, I was with him for thirteen years, from high school to just a few days ago. That's like…half my life, with one man. He was wrapped in everything I did, everything I was." I bit my lip, trying to keep the emotions back. "It's been hard sorting him out of my thoughts, out of my decisions. I've been just not thinking about him, since I'm so angry at him. But…really, if I look deep, and hard, I realize I was unhappy. I just didn't understand it, or see it, until after everything happened."

Luca reached for my hand. "You can talk about it, Delilah. I will not be hurt, or upset. You need to talk about your feelings." I must have smirked at the idea of a man telling me to talk about my feelings, because he laughed and squeezed my hand. "Do not laugh at me. I am not saying I am so good at this for myself, but I know it is needed to be healthy. You have had your life upended. I am your friend, first and most importantly."

This made my eyes burn and sting. I blinked furiously and squeezed his hand. When I could breathe again, I said, "Thank you, Luca. That means a lot to me. I don't know what to say, though. I just have to keep moving, one day at a time. I've been pretending, even to myself, that I don't care, that I'm too angry to care. But now that it's been a few days…I'm hurt. I gave half my life to the bastard. He was my first and only sexual partner, until I met you. It never even crossed my mind that he might be cheating on me."

Luca nodded, his eyes hard. "To be cheated on is difficult. I know this, too, from my own experiences."

"It just keeps making me wonder what's wrong with me, that I wasn't enough for him."

Luca glanced at me, lifted my knuckles to his lips. "No, *mia bella*. You must not think this. I, too, wondered the same thing when Lia told me she had been sleeping with someone else. 'Why am I not good enough?' I asked myself, over again and over again. But in time I came to know that it was not me, not my fault. I loved her, and did all that I could for her. But what you must know within your heart and mind is that for some people, there is nothing that will ever be enough."

I shrugged. "It's just…the woman I caught him with…she was older than me, and, objectively speaking, not very attractive. But she was—she was skinny."

"Delilah, you cannot think—"

"I'm not hung up on that, really. At least, not much. It's hard not to be, at least a little bit. I'm not skinny, never have been, never will be, and I'm fine with that. I like who I am and what I look like. But, when you catch your husband in bed with a skinny old hag with floppy titties, it's hard not to think he picked her over you because you're not skinny."

"He picked her over you because he is an idiot," Luca said. "They say that some men only think with their dicks, but I think these kind of men, the ones who leave or cheat on amazing, beautiful women, they do not think at all. They only do what they think in the very moment they think it. It is thinking with instinct, but another word."

"Impulsive," I suggested. "I guess that fits Harry pretty well. He was kind of impulsive about things."

Luca pulled the car to a stop in little town off the main highway, where we ate some delicious food and shared a bottle of wine. It seemed odd to be drinking wine at noon, but it seemed perfectly normal to Luca, so I went along with it. I don't think Luca even felt anything from the glass and a half he drank, but I was filled with a warm buzz in my blood, a deep happiness settling over my shoulders like a blanket. The sun was shining, the sky clear blue, the air cool in the shade of the building.

"Would you care to take a walk with me?" Luca asked.

"Sure," I said.

Luca paid the bill and we set out, hand in hand. Luca had a blanket it in the back seat of his car, "for emergencies," he said, in case he ever had to sleep in the car. He folded it into a compact square and carried it under his arm. Beyond the little village where we'd eaten the land was lush, rolling hills and fields dotted with bursts of trees, scattered villages, and farms and vineyards. Luca led me away from the roads and the villages up into the forested hills, a gentle but strenuous hike away from civilization. Birds called, flapped, and trilled, and the wind soughed around us, clattering the leaves and cooling the sweat on my face.

After maybe half an hour of hiking, Luca stopped us on the crest of a hill beneath a tree with wide, leafy, overhanging branches, providing shade from the hot Italian sun. We lay down side by side on our backs, watching the clouds drift between the leaves.

Luca rolled to his side and rested a hand on my stomach. He didn't do anything further, but the look in his eyes told me enough. We were far from anyone, and I was feeling daring. I met his eyes and unzipped my shorts, shimmied them down, sat up, unhooked my bra, and stripped my shirt off. Being naked outside was a rush, another new experience.

Luca's fingers skimmed down my belly, across my thighs, brushed past my labia and then drifted upward. He didn't touch me sexually yet, running his hands over my skin, exploring every inch of my body. He stroked my arms, my hands, and my sides, cupped the curve of my breasts and my hips, glided his fingers over my thighs and calves and feet. Once he'd mapped my body with his hands, he did it all over again, but now with his lips.

I lay still and let him do as he wished, but with every touch of his hands, every hot, moist kiss of his lips, I felt my heart beating harder. This wasn't sex, somehow. What he was doing was more, was...intimate. Loving.

I felt the pounding in my heart take on the rhythm of fear: run, run, run. I didn't want him to love me. If he loved me, it would mean I'd have to love him back, and that was terrifying. I'd loved a man for half my life and been burned. I thought I knew him, thought I trusted him, thought he cared. It turned out I was wrong. I'd known Luca for barely forty-eight hours, and the idea that he could care enough to kiss and touch me so delicately, with such reverence...it sent shudders of fear rippling through my body next to the pleasure of his touch.

I didn't know what to do with it, what to say, what to feel. On the one hand, I was desperate to be touched, to be loved. The realization that Harry had been cheating on me probably for our entire relationship made every moment we'd spent together meaningless, empty, and worthless. He'd never loved me. So now, with Luca branding my flesh with his tender touch, I found I needed more, wanted more, even though it scared me.

Which was really confusing.

I didn't know whether to be afraid of the worship in Luca's eyes, or to melt into him because of it.

I was ruminating on this as he plied my body with fingers and mouth, and so wasn't prepared for his tongue to lap against my clit. I gasped in surprise, flinched, and then relaxed into his attentions. By now I knew his technique and was ready for it, prepared to feel the fireworks. And feel them I did. Oh, my, what ecstasy I found at the end of his tongue, the swirl of his fingers against my G-spot. I felt his mouth retreat as I began to near climax. I mewled, thrust my hips in an attempt to get his tongue back to my folds. I lifted up to see what he was doing, saw him spit into his fingers, smirk at me, and then lower his hands to my folds. I was already wet, already slick with his spit and my own juices, so I wrinkled my brow in confusion. Before I could ask what he was doing, however, I felt the answer. He pushed my thighs apart, spread the globes of my ass apart with one hand and then slipped his spit-slick fingers against the knot of muscle deep inside, the one place on my body I'd never, *ever* been touched. I gasped, tried to pull away, squeezed my legs together.

"Please, just relax. You will enjoy it, I promise you." Luca looked at me across the expanse of my body. "But if you don't want me to, I won't."

I was still tensed, watching him, considering. It went against everything, every unwritten rule in my life. But he hadn't done anything I didn't like yet, and I knew he wouldn't do anything to hurt me. I barely knew him, but I trusted him. Which also worried me. I'd known Harry forever, and I'd thought I could trust him.

But Luca wasn't Harry.

I relaxed my legs, closed my eyes, and waited.

He massaged in slow, gentle circles at first, and his tongue found my clit again, and his other fingers delved inside my pussy to stroke my walls. Sensations overloaded me, wired through me. He continued to massage in circles, and I felt his finger slip in past the ring of muscle. It wasn't unpleasant. Then, as his fingers and tongue worked their magic on my pussy, I began to feel the fiery pressure of climax rising and building, but...twice as potent as ever before. And it was just beginning.

Moans escaped past my lips, and my hips writhed. Luca's finger pushed deeper and then deeper yet, and now I was whimpering nonstop, explosions rocking through me, my lower half shuddering, and his finger was slipping out ever so slightly and pushing back in.

Then the climax washed over me in full, and my world shattered. I screamed. Lights burst behind my eyes, my body buzzed and tingled and shook, and still I came. When I thought I couldn't come any harder, I felt Luca slide his body up mine, still clothed. I ripped at his pants, his shirt, got him naked in record time. Still trembling with the rippling currents of orgasm, I felt Luca drive into me, thick and stretching me. I wrapped my body around him, clutched him close and rocked my hips into his, driving him deeper.

I lost track of time then. We might have been writhing together for minutes or hours; I'll never know. It was one long orgasm for me, an endless climax rising higher and higher until I couldn't withstand it any longer, until I could only hold tight to Luca and ride the ever-cresting wave of ecstasy, drowning, gasping.

When Luca finally slowed his thrusting and began to plunge into me with slow, primal force, I was nearly limp and still climaxing, slipping down the far slope of orgasm. And then he came, shuddering, growling, and cursing in gasps. When I felt him come, my body clenched around him one last time.

The sun was significantly lower in the sky when we woke. We dressed and hiked back to the car, holding hands.

When we were driving again, Luca turned to me. "So, what did you think?"

I knew what he was talking about. I smiled at him, shyly. "It was...intense."

"This is a good thing?"

"Holy shit, Luca. I've never felt anything like it in my life."

"Ah, then it is a good thing. I am glad." He took my hand and rubbed a thumb in circles around my knuckle. "Perhaps we can do it again, later?"

"I might need a shower first, though."

"At my parents' house you will be able to."

I didn't answer, only nodded. He was assuming I would stay with him there, it seemed. I wasn't so sure, though. There were so many doubts, so many worries about awkward questions, and expectations...none of which had any answers.

I didn't have long to consider, though, because less than an hour later we were twisting through the streets of Florence...Firenze. Luca parked his car and pulled my suitcase from the hatch, and led me through alleys and narrow side streets. We came to a wide wooden door that opened directly onto the street. Luca knocked once, then opened it and led me through. On the other side of the door was a wide courtyard, open to the air, windows on three sides and a fountain splashing in the center.

"Luca? *È voi*?" An older woman appeared, clearly Luca's mother, evident in the curve of their mouths and their aquiline noses.

"Yes, Mother, it is me," Luca responded, in English. He embraced his mother, kissed both her cheeks, and then turned to me. "Mother, this is Delilah, a very good friend of mine."

His mother smiled, looking at the way Luca and I stood close to each other, brushing but not touching in the casual closeness of people comfortable with each other's bodies.

"*E lei è solo un amica?*" Her smile was knowing, but friendly.

"English, Mother, please. Delilah is still learning to speak Italian." He nudged me forward, and I extended my hand to shake his mother's. "Delilah, this is my mother, Domenica."

"It's great to meet you, Domenica," I said. I wished I knew enough Italian to greet her properly, in her own language, but I was afraid what little I did know I would butcher.

"It is my own pleasure to having you here," Domenica said, taking my hand.

So maybe it wouldn't have mattered if I butchered it a little.

"*Grazie per avermi qui,*" I said.

Domenica smiled at me, nodding. She led us under an archway, down a narrow hallway lined with painted portraits and Virgin Marys. We ended up in a kitchen, wide, high-ceilinged, tiled walls and a fan beating slowly high above. A table sat near one wall, a long, thick slab of wood, scratched and battered and worn smooth over the gouges. It was clearly an ancient thing, much loved, much used. Domenica trailed a hand along the surface of the table as she passed.

"Sit, sit, please. Coffee will be served in *un momento*."

The chairs were just as old, solid and smooth worn. Luca sat next to me and held my hand under the table, which made me feel like a teenager. His mother bustled around the kitchen, filling a glass-and-metal carafe with water and coffee and setting it on a burner on the stove. It took a few moments to realize she was making coffee with a percolator, something I'd heard of but never seen. While the percolator was percolating, she set about making sandwiches, cutting thick slices of bread from homemade loaves, cutting meat from a haunch on a platter in the olive-green circa-1950 refrigerator, and cheese from a yellow-orange wheel. She set them in front of us. Luca's had the crusts cut off and set aside on the plate. I smirked at him.

"What?" He said, his mouth full. "Mama knows how I like my sandwiches. I have told you, I am a mama's boy."

"*Nessun'altra donna conosce un uomo come sua madre*," Domenica said, over her shoulder.

"Mother, quit playing ignorant. Speak English, please. It is rude." He turned to me. "What she said was, no other woman knows a man like his mother."

"I figured it was something like that. I caught *madre*."

Luca laughed, and then scowled at his mother as she muttered something else in Italian.

"She thinks it is funny to pretend to not know English. She understands every word we're saying, and she can speak it passably well, but she doesn't like to. She likes it when Americans underestimate her, I think."

Domenica glared at Luca, muttering what sounded suspiciously like curses at her son.

"Now she is being impolite. Saying such nasty things to her favorite son."

"Not favorite when you are so nosy," Domenica said, in heavily accented but fluent English. "So unkind to your age-old mama. Cannot let a woman have her secrets from American girlfriend."

"Mama, she is not my—I mean, we are not—" Luca stopped, pinched his nose. "Meddling old woman. Do not mind her, Delilah."

"I think she's funny," I said.

We finished the sandwiches, which were beyond delicious, and Domenica brought the percolator and set it on the table. She pushed the plunger down slowly, then poured the thick black coffee into old glazed-porcelain mugs. The coffee, even after milk and sugar, was strong enough to shock me with every careful sip.

Domenica sat down across from us, poured herself a mug of coffee, and sipped it, black. "You are on a holiday, Delilah?"

I nodded. "Yes, ma'am. A sort of...extended vacation, I guess."

Domenica's eyes narrowed. "You are looking for something, then?"

"Mama, please," Luca growled.

Domenica gazed at her son with wide-eyed interest. "Only I am asking questions." Voices echoed from the courtyard, a sudden bustle of noise and activity. "Ah, your brothers and sister are arrived here. I think maybe they need help, Luca? Delilah, you stay with me and help for making a dinner?"

"Mama, I don't think—"

"It's fine, Luca. I would like to help." I put a hand on his shoulder, standing up. Domenica turned away and busied herself with filling a pot of water, and I used the opportunity to sneak a surreptitious kiss. "Go, see your family. I'll be fine."

Luca swallowed the last of his coffee and stood up. He kissed me again, and as he turned away, he pinched my bottom. I stifled a squeak, leaping away from his hand, slapping him on the shoulder.

You'd think, having just been fully and incredibly sated by Luca, that I'd be fine for awhile, but as he walked away I found myself wondering how I could get him alone. I was worried by the depth of my desire for Luca and the hunger with which I wanted his body and the sweet heights of climax he took me to. I'd gone my entire life not knowing what I was missing, and now that Luca had shown me, I couldn't get enough.

I turned away and attended to Domenica, who, with a knowing glint to her eye, ignored the exchange between Luca and me. She directed me in helping her prepare an elaborate spread of food, pasta, homemade sauce in clear mason jars, some kind of dish with sautéed chicken and roasted red peppers, steamed vegetables...too many other dishes and sides to remember or name. With the amount of food we were making, I found myself wondering exactly how many brothers and sisters Luca had.

As we began to finish the dishes, Domenica handed me a stack of plates and an assortment of battered, mismatched silverware. There was a formal dining room just off the kitchen, a long, narrow room containing a table meant for at least twenty people. I set the plates out, counting as I went. There were twenty-two places. Which meant, minus myself, there were twenty-one people in his immediate family.

I may or may not have had a minor panic attack as I arranged the silverware. I had one sister, and she had two kids. Harry was an only child. Even if both my family and his got together, we'd still only number ten. I tried to fathom twenty-one people at one table, from one family. Twenty-one.

What the hell had I gotten myself into, coming here?

I heard voices in the kitchen, all jabbering excitedly in Italian. I heard several male voices, several female, and a chaotic burst of children's voices. I made out Luca's honey-smooth voice among the babble, and felt a measure of peace knowing he'd be there with me. But...seriously? Twenty-one people? I'd never been with that many people at once except at parties in college, or classes. A family gathering? It wasn't even a holiday, as far as I knew. It was a Sunday in June.

I pushed away my nerves and set out the candles I found on a sideboard, huge white tallow tapers on elaborate silver candlesticks. There was a stack of linen napkins, and the sideboard also contained dozens of glasses of all shapes and sizes, mostly wine goblets of one kind or another of varying sizes. Not knowing what else to do, I set the wine glasses out at random.

I heard a footstep behind me, turned around, and felt Luca's arms wrap around me. His lips touched my jaw, my neck, and then my throat before moving up to my chin and sliding across my lips. His hands ran up my sides and back down, cupping my ass and pulling my body against his. I let myself melt into him, tried to draw strength from his steady heartbeat and graceful strength.

"Your heart is hitting so fast in your chest," Luca murmured. "You are not afraid, are you?"

I nodded. "There's twenty-one places, Luca. That's all just your siblings and their kids?" Luca nodded. "It's so many people. I don't...my family is small, and we don't all get together at once very often. And I just met you, and..."

"Delilah, please, you need to calm down. We are just a family. I did not think of us as so many people, but I can see your fears. My family is kind. They will like you. You will be right at home, I promise. All of my brothers and sisters speak English, and most of their children do as well. You will be fine." Luca looked at the table. "You did very nicely putting out the settings. Mama will approve."

"I wasn't sure about the glasses. They all seemed to be the same, so I..."

"It is fine. They are just things to drink from. No need to worry for it." He pulled my hand to lead me back into the kitchen. "Just be your wonderful self, *mia bella*. It will all be fine."

It seemed we had arrived a little bit before everyone else. The kitchen, which had before seemed so spacious, was now filled with chattering people, lilting Italian, and laughter and voices raised in voluble excitement. Children ranging in age from early teens to barely toddlers ran in and out of the kitchen, chasing each other and shrieking. I counted eleven, but they all looked alike and they wouldn't hold still, so I couldn't be sure.

Luca held my hand as we entered the kitchen. Hand-holding seemed to send a pretty clear message as to the nature of our relationship; I considered taking my hand back, but I honestly needed the reassurance of his hand in mine. The only way I would make it through this evening was with Luca.

A child of about six or seven, a cute little boy with unruly black hair and wide brown eyes, stopped in front of us, regarding me with naked curiosity. "Are you Zio Luca's girlfriend?" he asked.

I froze, blinked several times. Was I? I decided to go with the easiest answer.

Luca opened his mouth to answer, but I beat him to it. "Yes, I am," I said in English. I tried an Italian phrase: "*Come si chiama? Il mio nome è Delilah.*"

"Delilah? I like this name. I am Benito. You are Americano?" He seemed eager to try his English. "Do you have a television in your bathroom?"

I tried to hide my puzzled look. "Um, no, I only have a TV in my living room."

I pushed away the thought that I didn't have a living room, or a TV, anymore.

"Why is your hair red? I met a lady with red hair. She was from Irish-land. She was fat and old. You are pretty and young. Your hair is not so red like hers. Hers was *arancione come carote*. Can I touch your hair?"

Luca ruffled the boy's hair, saying, "Benito, you are such a trouble-making boy. Leave Delilah alone and go play *con i vostri cugini.*"

I laughed. "No, it's fine." I knelt down and tipped my head toward him.

He rubbed a lock of hair between his fingers, as if the red color might come off. He laughed, ruffled my hair like Luca had his, then ran off. I stood up, running my hands through my hair to smooth it.

"I am sorry about him. He is my brother's son, and he is truly a troublemaker, but he only means well."

"It's fine. He reminds me of my nephew at that age. Curious, and says anything that pops into his head."

"You have a nephew?" Luca asked.

I nodded. "And a niece. They're teenagers now. Lucy and Raymond."

Again, unwelcome thoughts pushed into my head. I didn't think I could ever talk to my sister again. If I saw her, I'd completely lose it. If I saw her husband, I'd tell him she was a cheating whore, and then he'd have a heart attack, and it'd be my fault, so I probably wouldn't ever see my niece and nephew again. I thought of Lucy with her bright blonde hair, her volleyball uniform, and Justin Bieber T-shirts, and then Raymond with his godawful death metal shirts and shaggy hair and earbuds always in his ears. My eyes stung. I blinked hard, rubbed at my eyes as if they itched.

Luca wasn't fooled. "What did I say?"

I shook my head. "Nothing. Just thinking of my niece and nephew."

"You miss them?"

"Yes. I will miss them very much."

"You will? What do you mean? Won't you see them again when you go back to America?"

I shrugged. "I don't know. I'm not sure I want to go back, for one thing. And I could never face my sister again, even if I did."

Luca looked puzzled. I hadn't told him about my sister and Harry. I sighed. "She slept with Harry."

"I thought you found him with an older woman? A preacher's wife or some such."

We were standing in the corner of the kitchen with his family buzzing around us. A giant bottle of wine had been opened and glasses were being poured and passed around, even to some of the older children. I sipped my wine and wished this hadn't come up.

"I did. When I found them, I packed my bag and left. I stopped by my sister's work, thinking I would talk to her. But when I saw her, and told her what I'd found, I just...I realized." My voice lowered until Luca had to lean close to hear. "My own sister, Luca. The bastard slept with my sister.

And she—you know what? No. I don't want to talk about this now."

Luca wrapped his arm around my shoulders. "No, truly. I am sorry to have brought up bad memories. Drink some wine. Come, perhaps I can persuade my sisters to play music so we might dance. Hmm?"

He tugged me by the hand through the house and into a living room stuffed with couches and chairs and love seats and an upright piano underneath a window. Children played on the floor with toys spilling out of a wicker basket. Four women sat clustered on the chairs around the children, chatting in Italian. When Luca and I came in, they all stood up and hugged and kissed him. He introduced me to them: Lucia, his older sister; Elisabetta, his younger sister; Giuliana, his sister-in-law; and Marta, his other sister-in-law.

They all effused volubly about how wonderful it was to meet a friend of Luca's and how nice it was for me to join them for their family dinner. I smiled and agreed. They were physical, these women, lunging in and hugging me, wine glasses sloshing but not spilling, kissing my cheeks. I resisted the urge to wipe my face. I hadn't been kissed on the cheek by a woman since I was a little girl, and I hadn't liked it then. I liked it even less as an adult, being kissed by women I'd known for five seconds. I mean, sure, it's a European custom, but when the custom is happening to you and you're not ready for it, it comes as a bit of a shock.

I was saved from further awkwardness by Luca's mother announcing it was time to eat. Dinner was chaotic, loud, fun, filling, and delicious. Everyone passed the dishes around in an endless circle, everyone talked all at the same time, children shouting to each other from across the table, adults doing the same, everyone laughing, wine flowing like water, even the little children sneaking sips under their parents' watchful gazes. I could only eat quietly, take in the insanity, and try to imagine growing up in such huge, close-knit family. When I was growing up, dinner was a largely silent affair. Mother portioned food out for us before we sat down, we drank water or milk, and we didn't talk during dinner unless directly addressed.

This...this was total lunacy. Food was shoveled in as fast as you could eat it, seconds and thirds were taken without asking, dishes passed and set down and passed and refilled, forks and knives clattering in a constant undercurrent beneath the incessant chatter of conversations, all in rapid-fire Italian.

Even Luca seemed to forget my presence for the most part, holding a nearly shouted conversation with a middle-aged man across the table, one of his brothers or brothers-in-law, I assumed. Domenica was at one end of the table, and her husband was at the other, a dignified older man with thick, mostly gray hair, wrinkled, leathery skin and kind, deep-set gray eyes.

Questions were tossed at me every now and then. How did I like Italy, what did I think of Rome, did I see the Colesseum, and isn't Firenze the most beautiful city I'd ever seen, and how long was I here, and what did I do when I wasn't on holiday? I tried to answer them, smiled, and kept eating. The meal lasted for over an hour, people eating, eating, eating, taking a break to swill wine and let the food settle and talk, talk, talk, and then eating more, until all the food, which I'd thought could feed an army, was gone.

There wasn't any one moment or signal, but everyone stood up and worked together to clear their plates and glasses and the dishes. I found myself at the sink with Marta, a sister-in-law, washing plates while she rinsed, and the other sisters dried and put them away. They spoke English to me, wondering how I'd met Luca. I tried to avoid the questions, but they were insistent, so I told them about my bag being stolen and Luca getting it back. They seemed to find this funny and cute and romantic and totally in character for Luca.

"He must really like you," Elisabetta said.

Elisabetta was younger than me by maybe three years, with black hair braided over her shoulder to hang between her ample breasts. She was built like me, with wide hips, large breasts, a little taller than average, a little heavy, but she wore her curves with a delicate grace and elegance that I envied.

"Why do you say that?" I asked.

She grinned at me. "Well, you are here, are you not? Luca does not often bring people to Sunday dinner. I don't know if he ever has."

I frowned. "He said you guys brought people over all the time."

Elisabetta and Lucia exchanged a look I couldn't quite decipher.

"No, that is not quite true," Lucia said. "I am not so sure why he would say that. Perhaps you heard him wrong? When we were younger and not married, perhaps it was true, when we had a boy-friend to introduce to the family. If he couldn't find a comfortable place with Elisabetta and the boys, then he wouldn't get another date with us. Family is the best test of finding a fitting mate."

Lucia was taller than the rest of us, thin and willowy, her hair a little thinner and finer, her fingers long and restless, much like Luca's.

Elisabetta nodded, and so did Marta.

"I did the same with Lorenzo," Marta said. "If he couldn't be friends with my brothers, I knew he couldn't be my husband." Marta's English was the most fluent, accented with a hint of British pronunciation, as if she'd spent time in England.

I was silent through these exchanges, the women trading stories of their husbands learning to get along with their families. My heart was thudding.

"So you think he's testing me?" I asked.

Elisabetta laughed. "I think he likes you. That is what I think. Testing? I do not know if this is true. But you are here, and you are a sweet girl whom I like. So you should not worry about it, hmm?"

Lucia seemed to sense my worry. "Don't think of it. If you have worries, tell Luca. He will tell you the truth." She smiled at me as she wiped her hands dry on a rag.

When the clean-up was done, we found the men and the children all gathered in the courtyard. The children were kicking a soccer ball around, and the men, glasses of wine and liquor in their hands, would occasionally deflect a rogue kick. Luca was the most active, darting between children to steal the ball, passing it, laughing and playing as if he was a child himself. I stood near the entryway of the courtyard, watching him play with the kids.

He will make a good father. The thought passed through my head like a bolt of lightning. It was true, and obvious. He was clearly comfortable with the kids, as easy with the teenagers as the youngest toddlers. Even as I thought this, he scooped up a little girl, not even two, probably, toddling around and shrieking, trying to keep up with the big kids and getting frustrated when her little legs would trip her up. Luca lodged the girl on his shoulders and leaped around the courtyard, kicking the ball, laughing when the girl tugged on his hair to get him to go a different direction.

He really would make a good father. The thought in itself was simple and innocuous enough. The part that troubled me was that the thought also came with a vision of him romping around a similar courtyard with a little girl that happened to have vivid cerulean eyes like mine, above an aquiline nose and straight, jet-black hair. That bothered me. Why did I see that? I didn't want kids. I saw what Leah went through with Lucy and Raymond, the hellish experience of birth, all the blood and screaming…I mean, yeah, Leah says it was worth it and you sort of forget it all once you hold the baby in your arms, but I'm not sure I believe her. The way she was screaming when Ray came out, that's not something you forget, no matter how cute the kid is. And I also remember how haggard Leah looked for months after the birth, the dark circles under her eyes, the way she moved as if she'd gone beyond exhaustion into something else.

So…why am I thinking of kids? With a man I just met? It's complete lunacy. Idiocy. Madness. I've gone crazy.

I looked up at that moment to see Luca's piercing brown eyes locked on mine, his little niece in his arms, giggling wildly as he tickled her, blew raspberries into her belly.

"He is so good with the children, no?" Lucia said, appearing next to me. She handed me a little glass of something clear and potent, like vodka. "It is grappa, from the vineyard for whom Luca is employed."

"He is good with the kids, yes."

"He has had plenty of practice. There are eleven of them, the nieces and nephews for him. He is the only one not married yet. Mama wants him to give her the next grandchild, but he says he is not ready." She took a swallow of grappa, wincing at the bite. "He might have been, if Lia had not hurt him so badly."

"He mentioned her, but we didn't really talk about it," I said. I wasn't sure I wanted to have this conversation with Lucia. Such discussions usually result in things being said that someone doesn't want aired.

"Well, there is not much to tell," Lucia said. "He was so young when they married, only twenty-two, I think. She was older than he, by a matter of some five years. She was very sweet, very kind, or so it seemed. Everyone liked her, except me. I was not so sure why not, but something about her made me...not so trusting."

I choked on my grappa. "They were married?" I tried not sound as peeved as I was.

"Oh, yes, for a few years, too. Happy, they seemed. Then, she left. No reason given to him, no letter or note or a phone call or nothing. Only an empty apartment." Lucia watched her brother, the memory of his pain and her love for him communicated in the glint of her eyes. "He was broken in his heart. He loved her very much, you see, and when Lia left, of course she took Luisa with her."

A stone of dread hit my stomach. "Luisa?"

"Such a delightful child, Luisa was. Hair like the wings of ravens, and so very bright."

"There—there was a…a child?" I could barely whisper.

Lucia look at me with concern. "*Merda*. He has not told you this, has he?" She put a hand on my arm; I jerked it away and stumbled along the wall toward the door leading to the street. "Delilah, wait, you do not understand. It is not like you think."

I wasn't listening. I set my glass of grappa on the arm of a chair and made my way to the door.

Had a child? And he hadn't told me? He had been married? God, I was an idiot.

"Delilah, wait, please," Luca was behind me, catching at my sleeve. "Lucia was mistaken to tell you what she did. You don't understand."

I shook my head and pushed the gate open. I was nearly flattened by a woman on a Vespa darting past me, and then a truck full of produce and fruit. I couldn't hear, couldn't see, only thought of getting away.

I heard Luca behind me, calling me. Eventually his voice fell away, but I felt his presence behind me. I didn't heed where I was going. Night had fallen by now, the city bathed in shadows and an orange glow from street lights and cafe noise. I came to a bridge, stopped, leaned over to watch the water flow beneath me. Luca stopped beside me, silent, waiting.

When I didn't speak, he moved closer to me. "Delilah, please listen. Yes, I was married. She left me, one year ago today, as a matter of fact. But I do not have a child. I promise you this."

I looked at him for the first time since leaving the house. "But Lucia said—"

"My sister means well, but she is sometimes rash with the things she says. Luisa was Lia's daughter, not mine. I—I cared for her, very much, but she was not my child. I thought...I thought she was, considered her to be, but when Lia left me, I realized she was not my daughter, and never would be again." He picked with a fingernail at the mortar between the stones of the ancient bridge. "I am sorry I did not tell you sooner, but truly, I did not think you would appreciate being burdened with my past dramas, when you have your own which you are seeking to heal from."

I felt the stone lift from my chest. "So you don't have a kid out there somewhere?"

"No!" Luca spoke vehemently. "If I had a child, I would be there, every day, every moment. I would not let the child be taken away from me. I would stop at nothing to be the father for that child. But Luisa, she was not mine. I had no rights to her, and if Lia did not want me, did not want our family any longer, I could not fight it. In truth, for all that it seemed to everyone we were so in love, so perfect together, it was not so. In private, Lia was a different person."

Luca seemed lost in his story now, and I didn't interrupt.

"She was so polite and friendly with my family, so seeming to be a model person, model member of this family." Luca shook his head, eyes downcast and glittering with old hurt. "In our home together, it was a much altered Lia I lived with. Unkind. Given to hard words, sharp words. Insults. Nothing I do could be enough to make her pleased. *Dio*, so angry. I never knew why. She kept her past a secret from me, but I was wise enough to see the scars of a life of pain, from before I met her. She told me one time, that she had slept with someone else. I have not told anyone this, not even my sisters. I forgave her, and tried to forget, but...it is not so easy. I tried to move on, but then, one day, I came back from a trip to sell *vino* in Marseilles and

Venice and Corsica, and she was gone. Just made vanished. Nothing to say to me why. Clothes gone, my car, gone. All of the money we save together, gone."

I didn't know what to say.

"Luca, I—I'm sorry." I put my hand on his back, rubbed in circles. "I'm sorry. I should have given you a chance to explain."

"I have explained, and now you know." Luca turned to put his back to the railing of the bridge, pulled me into him. "So, can we go back home now? The others are worried for you. Lucia feels poorly about it."

I let him lead me back to his parents' house. There were explanations of misunderstanding all around, and I spent a long time reassuring Lucia that everything had worked out just fine.

My grappa was put back in my hand, and I lounged on a bench with Luca as his family swirled around us, children laughing and chasing each other, kicking the soccer ball, the adults mingling. At some point, Elisabetta and Lucia produced instruments, a mandolin for Lucia and a violin for Elisabetta. They tuned, discussed for a moment, then struck up a lively jig. Everyone joined in, turning the courtyard into an even more chaotic scene, people now dancing in circles, swinging and spinning in circles, everyone making up their own dance steps.

I felt my feet tapping, my body wanting to move. Aside from writing, I've always loved dancing. It was an activity that I seldom got to do, however, as small towns aren't exactly known for their night life. In college, however, I took classes nearly every day, mostly classical ballroom stuff, tangos and waltzes and samba and such. The more interpretive styles like jazz and contemporary didn't appeal to me as much. I liked the stylized steps, the ordered beauty.

Luca looked at me sidelong. "Do you dance?"

I shrugged, smiling shyly. "A little."

He stood up, held out his hand, and I took it, let him pull me to an open area. He started off easy, a basic waltz hold, and trotted around with me, no steps, no structure. The sisters shifted their song, playing a tune I'd danced to frequently during ballroom classes, and automatically adjusted my hold on Luca, my feet starting the steps on their own. Luca's face showed his surprise, but he went with it, his spine going rigid, his hold formal and elegant, his feet light and quick.

Good gravy, the man could dance. My instructors had always told me I could have had a future in ballroom dancing, if I'd been willing to put the work in and slim down a bit. Good thing I liked writing more, since slimming down never seemed to work. A bit of a digression, there. My point is, I can tell the difference between someone who simply likes to dance, and someone who has had training, who takes it seriously.

Luca was a dancer. His poise was impeccable, his mastery of footwork breathtaking. He led me flawlessly, moving me around the courtyard, our eyes locked, the world blocked out but for the music flowing between us and in our veins. We came to a part of the dance where there would normally be a lift, if this was a choreographed number. I felt Luca's hold adjusting, watched his eyes scan the floor around us, calculating, assessing.

"Ready?" he breathed.

I nodded. Three steps, a half-turn, and then his hands moved to my waist, lifting me as I hopped. I'm not the most agile girl in the world, but I'm lighter on my feet than most people would assume, and Luca, well, he was powerful enough to lift me and make it look effortless.

We pulled off the lift like we'd practiced it for days. I felt the rush of excitement and adrenaline that follows pulling off something difficult, and then we were off again, spinning around the courtyard, his hand hot and powerful on my waist, his eyes piercing mine, desire raging from him in palpable waves, igniting my own need and lust. Dancing had suddenly never been so sensual, our bodies moving in perfect harmony, fitting just right.

The song eventually ended, and Luca and I glided to a stop, hand in hand, breathing hard and sweating, unable to break eye contact. His family was cheering, clapping, the kids going wild. I realized they'd all stopped to watch, and felt my cheeks flame. I'd never danced for an audience. I took lessons, got my fix out then, and never had any desire to get on a stage and perform, or compete, even though my instructors fairly begged me to on a regular basis.

"You are a truly marvelous dancer, Delilah," Luca said.

"You, too. I had no idea you were a dancer."

"Nor did I." Luca led me by the hand out of the courtyard and away from the prying eyes of his family. "We should dance together more often. I have not danced with someone so skilled in many years."

"Me, either," I said. "Not since college. I can't believe we did that lift!"

Luca laughed. "I know! I thought it was worth a try, when I realized you knew the steps so fluently. You are very graceful."

We were standing near a flight of stairs, and Luca glanced from my flushed face to the stairs, and then the courtyard. His family was dancing again, Elisabetta and Lucia playing another improvised jig.

Luca licked his lips, and then pulled me up the stairs.

"Where are we going?" I asked. I hoped he had in mind what I thought he did.

"Somewhere private. Or, mostly private." Luca turned a corner, pulling me down a narrow, wood-paneled hallway to a door at the end.

The room behind the door was small but comfortable, a guest bedroom obviously seldom used. There were two windows, one looking out over the city, and the other over the courtyard. The music was clearly audible, the laughter of children mingling with the chatter of adults, the slap of feet against cobblestones and the splashing fountain.

Somehow, my suitcase was in the corner of the room. I wasn't sure when Luca had brought it in from the car, but there it was.

Luca closed the door and hooked a chain over the door, then turned to me, desire fiery in his eyes. I lunged for him, locking my lips around his, my hands pulling at his shirt, tugging it off, and then unbuttoning his jeans. A flurry of busy hands had both of us naked in seconds, and then Luca's warm hands were skimming over my body, mine over his.

His mouth trailed kisses down my throat to my breasts, teeth grazing my nipples, and then his fingers slipped over my belly to caress the mound of my sex, unleashing a flood between my thighs. His cock was hard in my hands, an intoxicating shaft of heat and steel and silk.

I wanted him, right then. I didn't want to wait for him to touch me. I moved toward him, lifting on my toes, guiding him toward my entrance. Luca had other plans. He pushed me back toward the bed, kissing my lips hard enough to take my breath away. I started to crawl backward on the bed, but Luca gave me a mischievous grin, then took my hips in his hands and turned me around to face the bed. I looked at him over my shoulder, confused.

He ran his hands up my back, caressing and pushing at the same time, then pressed his lips to my spine, tangled his fingers in mine and stretched my arms over my head. Somehow I ended up bent forward over the bed, my arms in front of me. I began to understand what he had planned when his hands moved back down my spine toward my ass, then down farther still to stroke my pussy with gentle, probing fingers. He found my entrance and delved in with his fingers, curling up to find my G-spot, caressing it until I began to move my hips and gasp.

I felt the leaking tip of his cock drag down the crease of my ass, guided by his hand, and then he was sliding inside me, filling me, pushing deep. He was standing straight, his cock buried inside me, and then he pulled back and drove in, and I couldn't help moaning low in my throat.

"Shhh, the window is open. They will hear us," Luca whispered. "Not a sound, okay?"

I nodded and bit the blanket as he moved in a rhythm within me, thrusting harder with every passing second, on hand braced on my lower back, the other pulling my hips back into him. I felt his finger trace down my ass, slip between the cheeks and probe the knot of muscle there. Something wet and warm touched my second opening and then his finger was pushing in, slowly and carefully. Now I was ready for it, knew what it would feel like, welcomed it with an eagerness that worried me in the back of my head.

His finger slipped in, and I had to stifle another loud moan. I felt myself stretch again back there, and then the filled feeling increased and my rising orgasm neared peak. I craned my neck to look over my shoulder, but all I could see was Luca's body moving as he plunged into my pussy.

"I would like to put myself down there," he said, leaning over to whisper into my ear. "Do you trust me to do so?"

"You mean, your...you want to put your cock...in there?" The idea filled me with panic all over again.

Luca nodded, and I hesitated.

I was just getting used to his fingers. I liked his fingers, liked the intensity of the orgasm it gave me, but I wasn't sure I was ready for any more, either physically or mentally.

"I don't know, Luca. I'm kind of nervous about that. Especially with the window open." I felt his fingers withdrawing. "You can keep doing what you're doing, but...can we wait for...the other part? I'm not saying no, just not yet. Not now."

"It is okay," he said. "I hope I did not upset you."

I shook my head and moved my hips back into him. "No, no. Just...don't stop. Keep going. I'm close."

He kissed my back, rolled his hips into my ass and filled me, deep and slow. I moaned into the mattress as the climax, which had started to recede with the distraction, began to build up again. Luca's body moved against mine in a slow and steady rhythm, his hips bumping against the flesh and muscle of my backside, his muscled thighs brushing against mine, his hand on my hip and two fingers slipping deeper into my ass with every thrust of his cock.

Sensation swept over me, inundated me. I was being stretched and filled, pushed to the brink of tolerance, so full of Luca, so burning with the raging fire of boiling climax that I nearly couldn't take it anymore, almost wanted to tell him to stop, to take his fingers out and let me come with him on my back, in a more familiar position. I wasn't uncomfortable, standing bent forward, but it was so new, so unfamiliar, so strange. The only contact

between us was sexual, and I had gotten to like…
to love…the feel of his body on mine, his broad,
dark bulk pinning me and protecting me, shelter-
ing me.

This…this was different. I was presented as a
sexual object like this. Only his cock inside me, his
fingers inside me, his hands encouraging me. Did
I like this? I had to ask myself the question. It felt
good—I couldn't and wouldn't deny that. But…
did it feel good emotionally?

God, yes. It felt dirty. It felt wanton. It was
sinful.

While I debated this internally, I had slowed
the roll of my hips into him, let his body do the
work. Now, as I came to the decision to stop ques-
tioning, I gathered the blanket into my fists and
arched my back, lifted up on my toes, sent myself
plunging back into his body, and now, with my
help, his cock speared deep into me and the pressure of climax blew through me, sending shocks
of fire and heat rifling through my body. I buried
my face in the bed and let myself moan, let myself
whimper and sigh as sweet, powerful, thoughtful
Luca drove into me. I felt him cross the threshold,
that moment when he could no longer hold back,
could no longer keep his motions measured or his
thrusts gentle.

His fingers moved inside me, pushed deeper, and
then he was leaning forward and his knees were

trembling against the back of my legs and he was coming and so was I, grinding my teeth together to keep from crying out loud. Luca's hand dug into my hip and jerked me backward as he powered into me, his balls slapping against me, his come shooting deep and his tip throbbing against my wall.

We came together, moving in sync, me thrust back as he pushed forward, slow, savage grinding of our bodies together, instinctively seeking to go deeper, more, harder. I heard his breath coming in ragged gasps behind me. The orgasm washing through me was like a tsunami of sensate delight, a true agony of ecstasy, too much thrilling raging rampant pleasure to contain, light bursting behind my eyes and in every synapse, every muscle clenching and releasing, clenching and releasing.

As Luca went limp on top of me, I wondered, if it felt that good to have his fingers down there, if I might like it even more with his manhood. I worried about it hurting, since his fingers, even two of them, were significantly smaller than his cock.

I knew then that I'd try it. I'd let him. I was glad I hadn't then and there, though, for I was learning I was vocal, and enjoyed letting myself shriek and moan out loud. Stifling my voice during sex seemed to dampen the pleasure I got from it, as silly as that may sound. The knowledge that we were within earshot of his entire family made the experience seem deliciously illicit and exhilaratingly naughty.

Luca slid out of me and helped me climb onto the bed, lay down next to me. "*Mio dio*, Delilah. The things you do to me."

I laughed. "I do to you? You're the one sticking your fingers in my asshole."

"True, but you liked it, I am fairly certain," Luca said, grinning.

"Oh, I liked it all right," I said.

He sobered. "I am sorry for pressuring you into something for which you were not ready."

I kissed him, just to reassure him. "You didn't pressure me, Luca. You asked, and I said not now, and you let it go." I traced circles with my fingertip in the light dusting of hair on his broad chest, not quite looking at him. "I'm willing to try, if you want. It's just...not here, not now. Not with everyone awake and listening, and whatever."

"No, you are right. This was perhaps not the best time for such things." He gave me a playful slap on the ass. "Especially since you make such loud, wonderful noises."

I blushed and buried my face against him again, my words muffled by his skin. "I am kind of noisy, huh?"

"Yes, and I love it."

There was an awkward tension suddenly, stemming from his use of the "L" word. Again, the panic hit me, and I tensed, my breath catching as if a weight had settled on my chest. Run. Run.

Run. My heartbeat was a rapid-fire thumping, and I wanted, in that moment, to get up, throw some clothes on, and flee, find a cab to anywhere. Love? No. No no no. I tried to tell myself he hadn't meant it like that, but it didn't help. I couldn't deal with being in love, being loved. I was in Italy to find myself, to figure out who I was, to get some life experience, some sexual experience. I was getting sexual experience in spades, and I was loving it, but the rest? Not so sure.

Who was I? Who was Delilah Flores? I knew I liked writing, and dancing. I liked wine. I liked sex, it seemed. I never really had before, it had just been something that happened because I was married and Harry was so damned persistent about it. But I'd never liked it, wanted it, needed it. Now, since meeting Luca, I couldn't get enough. Even now, barely ten minutes after a mind-blowing orgasm, I wanted Luca again.

So I liked sex, a lot.

A thought blew through my head. What would sex with Brad from Chicago have felt like? Would it have been different? What about someone else? A random man, someone from a different country, a different city? The body parts all went in the same places in the same way, so in some sense I thought it might all be pretty much the same. Right? But what if a different man was less understanding of my hesitancies? Less accepting of the fact that I wasn't a diminutive little thing? A different man may not have taken no as an answer just a few minutes ago.

If I let things with Luca progress and just stayed here in Italy with him, what possibilities would I be giving up? I had intended to see more of the world. Greece, England, Germany, Sweden, Ireland, there were so many places I wanted to see.

But Luca...god, he's amazing.

I'm sitting in the bed with him, with the window open and the sounds of laughter and conversation, all adult now as children begin to tire out. Luca is next to me, answering emails from his phone as I write. It's comfortable, intimate, and familiar. I can see myself doing this with him day in and day out, lying in bed together, writing, doing business, reading, talking, watching TV. The very fact that this seems so easy scares me. It's almost as if I'd always lain in bed with Luca, as if I always will.

The pressure of fear in my chest is back, leaning on me even as I type. I'm not sure what I want. I don't know what to do. So much of me is screaming at me to run, to flee, to catch a bus to the airport and fly away, go anywhere, don't get trapped by love before I've even begun my journey.

A niggling voice, small but insistent, says if I run, I could be giving up the best thing that ever happened to me.

Elisabetta is outside the door, telling us to come back out, we've had enough time alone.

This family seems like a family I could be very happy with. Which only serves to further confuse me.

June 16

I've spent the last two days in Firenze with Luca's family. I'm more at home with them than I've ever felt with my own family. Scary thought, huh?

Lucia in particular has become a close friend. Which leads into another scary thought: I didn't have any friends back home—back in the States. I mean, none. Leah was the closest thing, but she was my sister, and that doesn't really count, does it? I had work acquaintances, Harry, a few ladies from church that I'd do lunch with occasionally, but no one I could just sit around and drink grappa with, listen to music with, stroll the streets and chat with.

I do all these things with Lucia. She understands me in the same way as Luca. She doesn't judge me, she understands where I'm coming from emotionally, especially after I related my adventures of the past few days.

My god. It's only been a few days. Barely a week since I walked in on Harry with Helen. It's felt like a lifetime. I'm a different person already. I curse, I drink alcohol, and I have sex with Luca. A week ago, all these things would have been mortal sins, life-altering lapses in judgment. Here, it's just life.

My confusion isn't gone. I still don't know what to do. In the meantime, I stay here. It's easiest. Luca says he'll be here for at least two weeks, if not more, so there's no rush. I can take my time to decide. I'm not spending money on a hotel, or food, or cabs. I help Domenica cook, I help everyone clean up after meals, I play with the children. I'm learning Italian faster every day.

I want to see Venice. I want to see Athens, the Acropolis, millennia-old theaters where the first great plays were performed. I want to see London with the red double-decker buses and Big Ben and the London Bridge.

But, Luca. Lucia. Little Benito with his fast, loud mouth and adorable curls. Quiet little Rosa with her naked dolls and crayon drawings of ponies. Domenica, with her knowing eyes and effortless dignity and grace.

And Luca. Luca. His smooth power, quick, attentive hands, his skillful mouth. And god, his cock. I've never wanted anything so much, so frequently. I love being in bed with him. Or on the bed, or bent over the bed, or standing up against the wall (like this morning, as I was getting into the shower). Anywhere, anytime. I'm a monster for sex now. Poor Luca. I'm afraid I'm exhausting the poor man with my insatiable appetite.

But no, that's nonsense. He's as voracious as I am.

Here he comes now, back from the gym, sweaty, shirtless, hair splayed across his brow and sticking to his skin, muscles ripped and glistening, his cut-off sweat shorts hanging low across his hips, revealing that glorious V-cut of muscle. I think every woman likes that. Whether you like your men muscle-bound or wiry, hairy or smooth, that little indentation of muscles leading to his manhood is sexy and erotic in some kind of indefinable way. It just turns you on, gets you going and makes you salivate.

He's about to take my netbook from me. I'm sitting in bed in my panties and nothing else; I was about to take a shower and decided to journal instead, so now we're both raring to go.

I'll have to finish this later.

It's the middle of the night now, several hours after the preceding entry.

I've gotten addicted to writing these sex scenes, I think. I've read erotica books since I was in high school, my one lifelong dirty little secret. I could never quite make myself give them up, even though I always had a little twinge of guilt about them. But for some reason, whenever I tried to read a "normal" book, I found myself waiting and waiting for the sex, and it never came, and I was just frustrated and bored. So I'd go back to the erotica books.

This journal is a private thing. I'll never publish it, never let anyone read it. This is just for me. I look back at what I've written and I realize...some of it is actually pretty good. I get turned on reading the sexy bits. And...the more I continue this journal, the more I get into reliving the steamy scenes between Luca and me. It's like getting to do it all over again, and it makes the next time Luca and I have sex, make love—whatever you want to call it—that much sweeter and more potent.

So there I was, lying in the wide, springy bed, wearing nothing but a purple thong, my netbook on my lap, and Luca came in, fresh from the gym. I tried to pretend like I didn't notice him, like the only thing I saw was my screen, but the man knew better. He saw through my silly subterfuge and crawled across the bed like a predator through the grass. He took my laptop from me, set it on the floor, and then started kissing me, toes first, then my shins, then my thighs. When he came to my silk-covered mound, he put his mouth to the fabric and blew hot air against my opening. The heat and moisture of his breath did something strange, sent thrills of pleasure through me, made me instantly wet. I'm sure there's some cute and dirty name for that, but I don't know what it is.

Then he slid my thong by its string down around my hips and past my feet, threw it across the room. He paused, looking up at me with a sensual curve to his lips, a knowing smile that told me he knew exactly how much I enjoyed what he was about to do with his mouth.

He parted my thighs, bent down and kissed up my legs until his lips were touching my thighs and his cheek was brushing my labia with his stubble. Then he turned his lips to my sex, his tongue to my crevice, lapping at the folds, just the tip at first. He wrapped his arms around my hips and tugged me lower on the bed. I stuffed a pillow under my hips and tangled my fingers in his hair as he delved into my pussy with his tongue.

Oh, sweet mercy, anticipation makes it so much better. We'd gone this morning, a quick and dirty thing against the bathroom wall, satisfying its own way, hot and hard and lustful. This was so much different.

Slow and sweet and…I'm just not sure I have words for it all, but I'll try.

He didn't hurry. He lapped slowly at me, working me into a frenzy without ever moving his tongue any faster. Just slow circles at my clit, up and down, fingers curling in to stroke my G-spot in the same slow rhythm, another finger pressing the rosebud muscle of my anus, not entering but just slowly massaging, sending me into ecstasy-land.

I wondered briefly if he'd push the issue from earlier, regarding anal sex, but then forgot as he gradually increased his pace until I was thrashing beneath him, coming, coming, coming so hard. I dragged him up my body, pushed away his shorts and rolled him to his back.

I straddled him, still shuddering, lifted my quivering hips and drove him in, no hesitation, no slow entrance. I was wet, hot, trembling, ready. He slid in and we were off, moving together, me leaning back as far as I dared, until he was wincing. I wanted this to last, and I'd learned by now that if I leaned back it would keep him from coming until I relaxed the tension.

I didn't intend to let him come until he begged me. It wasn't about power, or wanting to control him. I just wanted to drag out the pure pleasure of having him inside me for as long as I could.

I moved as slowly as he had, rolling on him as if rocking on ocean waves, gentle swells. Luca put his hands on my thighs, thumbs near the crease where leg meets hip, fingers around the curve of my ass, not pushing or pulling, just resting, caressing. His head tipped back, his spine arched, his body lifted mine up, my shins taking my weight as I lifted and plunged, faster now, faster, deeper in and farther out.

"Luca, god, Luca." The words were pulled from me as if by a string connected to his soul.

"You are so beautiful, Delilah."

I melted. I wanted to collapse forward, but his breathing was harsh and panting, his body bucking, straining for release, and I was caught up in the drawing out of the pleasure, each thrash of his body driving him deeper inside me, my muscles trembling and tense and ready for the explosion, the implosion...

My hands braced on his stomach, propping me up, I rolled my hips onto his, ignoring his ever more vocal groans of need. Lean back, move faster, chemicals rushing, desire pounding, flesh burning and tangling with his, eyes closed now and all I knew was sensation.

"Delilah...*dio*, I am going to die if you do not let me come. I am going to burst, please..." Luca's voice was rough and raw and desperate.

I slid my hands up to his chest, keeping my hips tilted backward, my spine arched inward. Our eyes met, his burning and blazing with need, his fingers fiercely gripping my hips, pulling me forward. His cock thrust hard, his body bucking, each breath in and out a ragged groan.

I couldn't draw it out any longer. I'd already come, a gradual rising flood of climax. Now, with Luca so close, beyond the edge but held back from true release, I knew instinctively I'd come again, harder than ever, the moment I relaxed the tilt of my hips.

Luca growled, cursed in Italian, and then flipped me onto my back in a single motion. He was above me, suddenly, huge and hard and powerful and rocking into me. Oh, lord. He came with a rumble of relief deep in his chest. I wrapped my legs around his hips and pulled him into me, clutched his shoulder and the back of his head with shaking hands, feel orgasm wash over us, drive us together, push us past anything like mere physical release.

Luca's weight bore down on me, only his cock moving inside me, his breath hot in my ear, his hands tangled in my hair, his toes scrabbling at the blanket. I was coiled around him with serpentine strength, clinging to him, whimpering and whispering his name.

Something deep in my chest, incorporeal but integral to my identity, burst apart and flew out of me, into Luca, merged with him. I felt a joining then between us. The Bible verse "and they shall become one flesh" pulsed through my mind. I broke into sobs. I didn't know what was happening, what it meant, but I knew it was something I could never undo.

Luca was inside me, suddenly, emotionally and mentally, now. Not just physically, sexually, but the person of him was tangled with me. I knew, in that moment, I could never experience anything like this with anyone else. I was completely overwhelmed by physical sensation and emotional response, my body wracked with spasms.

Luca moved above me and in me, eyes locked with mine. His thumb wiped away the tears from my eyes, but he didn't ask why they were there. The glimmer of emotion in his eyes told me he knew exactly why.

It was too much.

When it was over and we were lying nestled together, I knew I would face a decision. There were no words between us, just a tacit knowledge of what we'd shared.

Eventually Luca's breathing evened out, leaving me awake, frightened, and confused.

That had gone far beyond mere sex. It threw every other moment we'd spent together into new perspective. It had never been "just sex" between us. Luca had been showing me what I'd been missing. He'd worshipped my body, given me something that went far beyond mere physical pleasure. He'd given me comfort with who I am, confidence in my own sexuality. It was a priceless gift.

So why was I about to run from again?

Sleep claimed me, briefly, fitfully.

I woke up again, about four in the morning, and started writing this entry.

The war is raging in my heart and head.

Run. Run. Run.

Love. Love. Love. It's there, Dee. This voice sounds oddly like Leah's, calm and practical. *Don't fight the love. Go with it. It's there, Dee, and you'd be a fool to run from it.*

He's so gorgeous. Look at him: longish black hair falling across his eyes, face so peaceful in repose, muscles bulky and powerful even at rest, the soft rise and fall of his chest like waves breaking on shore.

If I woke him and told him the war going on inside me, he'd find a way to soothe me, reassure me. I should wake him up. But I can't. He's so beautiful in his sleep, the thought of waking him up seems cruel.

But if he wakes up and finds me gone, he'll be heartbroken again.

Lord help me.

June 17

I'm in a train station in Geneva. It's noon. My heart is broken, for I know I've made the wrong decision. I ran. I packed my bag and left in the gray haze of dawn. I left a note this time.

Luca,

Please don't be angry. I'm sorry. I need space. I need time to think. I don't know what I want. Please don't think I left because of anything you did, or didn't do. You're wonderful and amazing. The problem is me. I'm still messed up, I guess, and things with you are just too incredible, too soon. I know that sounds stupid, but it's just overwhelming. I don't know where I'm going. I don't know what I'm doing. All I know is I'm sorry. I don't want to hurt you, and I hate the thought of how you'll feel reading this. I'll probably head north, into Europe. God, I'm rambling.

You're too good for me right now. I need time to be alone. I hope I'll be able to find you when I'm ready for things. If not, know that you gave me exactly what I needed.

Thank you. I'm sorry.

—Delilah

Before I left, I snooped in Luca's cell phone and found his number, copied it down so I could call him…someday.

The morning was cold and dim as I dragged my suitcase through the empty streets of Firenze… Florence. Firenze. Saying it in Italian was too hard. Florence. I heard Luca's voice, laughing and correcting my pronunciation.

I found the train station and got a ticket for Geneva, Switzerland. The train ride was long, slow, and beautiful. I missed Luca more with every mile that passed. Or, since I'm in Europe, every kilometer. I felt a part of my heart ripping out more and more as the train left Italy and moved north. I imagined Luca waking up, arm patting the empty bed beside him, thinking maybe I was just in the bathroom, or getting coffee, then finding the note. I imagined him crumpling the note, eyes glittering.

Would he come after me? Would he ask the train station attendant if he'd seen an American girl with red hair.

Did I want him to come after me?

Yes.

Could I turn around and go back? No. It would mean facing him, explaining even more. It was easier to make the break now. Break it off before I got hurt.

Well, shit. There's the truth. I'm afraid. I'm still hurting from Harry's betrayal, and I don't believe Luca won't hurt me, too.

June 18

Switzerland was incredible. Too perfect. Like Luca.

I left Switzerland behind today. I'm on another train, this one taking me to Belgium. Saw some Belgian sights, drank some Belgian beer. Took a bus to Prague. Lovely, ancient, incredible. In other circumstances I think I would have loved Prague.

Not like this.

What have I done?

June 20

Yesterday was the second worst day of my life. The worst one is pretty obvious, at this point. It's past noon, and I just woke up. I'm hung over. My head aches. My soul aches. My heart aches. I nearly made the worst mistake of my life.

Well, no. The worst mistake was leaving Luca, and that's one I can't undo, and I'm too much of a coward to go back and fix it. I can't face the heart-break and anger in his eyes a second time.

Cowardly me.

Yesterday I went to a club in Paris. I got sexy, put on too much makeup, wore too little clothing. Got drunk. Really, really drunk.

Met a guy named François. Lovely man. Shoulder-length blond hair, thin and wiry and not quite effeminate. An artist. Pale blue eyes, narrow shoulders, and manicured hands. Sharp features, a quick smile that didn't quite meet his eyes.

He plied me with white wine, sweet-talked me out of the club, into a cab, and back to his cramped, expensive loft apartment on Champs-Élysées. I know enough to know the little loft, which would have fit into my closet back in Illinois, was worth six of that house. I hated his loft. It was clean, neat, organized, expensive sound equipment and an enormous flat-screen TV and a deep leather couch taking up the entire loft. I wasn't sure where he slept. He sat me on the couch, handed me glass of something green and potent.

Absinthe, he called it. I went from drunk to something else. The world spun and flickered and wavered and flashed in strange washes of color. I felt François's hands on me, stripping my shirt off. I didn't like it. I couldn't get words out to tell him to stop, and I did kind of like it. I'd gone several days without sex, when I'd been making love to Luca several times a day for several days. I was hungry, ready. But it wasn't right. François was rough, clumsy. His nails scraped my sides as he ripped my shirt off. His fingers pinched my nipples through my bra, too hard.

No. The word wouldn't come out, and I couldn't figure out why.

The universe was shrinking down around me, narrowed to François and his pale, weak blue eyes, his strangely cruel fingers and his thin, piano-wire body pressed against mine. The walls should have been white, but they seemed at once blue and green and yellow, wavering in kaleidoscopic swirls.

Was there a drug in the strange green liquor he'd given me? I think there was. I thought it then, and even now, writing this in bed, waiting for room service to bring me coffee, I shiver and feel disgust writhing in my belly at the memory.

The thing that drove me into action was François digging between my clamped-closed thighs, manicured nails cutting the soft flesh as he sought my dry sex. He found it, pushed aside the negligible fabric of my panties, thrust a single finger into my vagina and tried to move it. I moaned in protest. He mistook it for pleasure, moved his finger harder, hurting me.

"NO!" The word burst from me, ripped free by the pain and the sense of violation.

I pushed him away, scrambled off the couch.

"Please, Delilah, wait. You are so beautiful. I want you, don't go, *mademoiselle*," Francois begged.

I slapped him, hard enough to spin him around and knock him to the ground. I found my shirt on the floor, hooked the straps of my high-heeled sandals in one finger and wove unsteadily out of his loft. I missed a step, fell down three stairs to the landing, hurting my backside and my tailbone. I refused to cry. The world spun, shook, distorted in awful crazed crayon-colors.

Nauseous. Disgusted. Afraid. Angry.

I found the street, hailed a cab. The driver was old, silver-haired and wrinkled and kindly-looking. He turned his face to the side, not quite looking at me, not asking where I wanted to go. I fumbled the card of my hotel from my purse, showed it to him.

He nodded. "*Oui. Immédiatement.*" His voice was gravelly, smoky.

I stumbled into my room, collapsed on the bed after latching the bar-lock on the door. I took a dozen deep breaths, shuddered, and then shattered into sobs. I fell asleep, the world still wobbling on its axis, colors wrong. Shame burned in my throat with the bile.

When I woke up, I knew I couldn't go on like this.

I've made a mistake, and I have to face it, fix it somehow. No more cowardly running across Europe.

The food is here. The young man pushing the cart reminds me of Luca in a way. Younger, but longish dark across his brow, thick shoulders, strong hands. I'm not wearing much, I'm suddenly realizing. I stripped off my clothes before passing out, and now all that covers me is the bed sheet. The young man is struggling gamely to not stare at me. I smile at him over the screen of my netbook.

He's not Luca. I break the eye contact and stare at my screen so he knows I'm not interested in anything else but the food. He thanks me in French, his dark gaze flickering to my breasts again and then away.

Finally he's gone.

The coffee and food smell great, but all I can think of is François and his hard fingers inside me.

I want Luca here.

I called Luca. He answered on the second ring, relief in his voice.

"Luca?" My voice was quiet, hesitant. "I...I'm sorry."

"No, Delilah. It is okay. I understand. Where are you?"

"Paris." I wanted to tell him what happened, but I can't. "I...can you come?"

"Stay where you are. I will be there as soon as I can. What is the name of your hotel?"

I told him. He didn't say anything else, just told me to stay in my room and wait.

Hours passed. I watched French TV, not understanding a word. I had a *New York Times* sent up and try to read it, but I found myself reading the same paragraph a dozen times without comprehending anything. Finally, I pulled out my netbook again and wrote, reread what I've written, going back the first page, composed in a cafe in Rome. Roma.

I can't believe the craziness that has become my life.

I miss George and José.

Luca is here. My heart is pounding like tympani in my chest.

Delilah's Diary 3: Sexy Surrender

June 21

MY HEART POUNDED IN MY CHEST as I twisted the knob and opened the hotel door. Luca stood with one hand in the pocket of his dark blue jeans, his black hair sweeping across his brow and in front of his eye. He brushed the stray strands aside with a callused thumb, his coal-dark eyes blazing with anger and hurt. For a long, tense moment, neither of us spoke, neither of us moved.

I clasped my hands in front of me to conceal their shaking. "Luca, I…" I stepped back, not quite able to meet his eyes. "Come in?"

Luca stepped past me and sat down in the chair near the window, arms crossed over his broad chest. His gaze was hard and inscrutable.

"Why did you leave me, Delilah?"

I shook my head. "It's...I'm sorry. I don't know."

"I think you do know."

I crossed the room and stood in front of him. "You read the note. That's why."

Luca snorted. "That was a childish excuse. Nothing more. It did not explain anything whatsoever."

"Well, then, what is it you want to hear?" I finally met his eyes, but they were still hard, angry, and, above all, hurt.

"I would like to hear the truth. No more excusing it behind nonsense and *merda*."

I felt a rush of irritation. "It's not shit, Luca. It is the truth. I don't know what this is between us, or how to deal with it. You make me feel things I've never felt before. It's frightening. It's all so soon after—after Harry. I'm not running from you, exactly, more from us, from how intense everything between us is."

"You think I will betray you as your husband Harry did?" Luca scratched at the knee of his jeans.

"*Ex*-husband. And no, not really. You've been betrayed before, and I don't think you'd do that to someone else. Besides which, I don't think you're like that anyway."

"But still you run away whenever things become too much between us."

I could only nod. Eventually, I was able to speak again. "You...you deserve better, Luca. You're just so amazing. And I'm—I don't event know who I am."

"I know who you are," Luca said, leaning forward. "You are Delilah Flores. You are beautiful, and brave, and so very complex, like a diamond with a million faces always changing and showing the world something new."

I shook my head. "We must see different people when we look at me." I frowned. "That didn't make any sense."

Luca laughed. "No, it did not, but I understood your meaning." He stood up, and his eyes were softening. I could still see the hurt and anger in the lines of his face, the crow's feet and the pinching of his eyebrows. "Nevertheless, that is what I see when I look at you. That is who I know when I speak to you. You must see it is as well."

"I don't know how."

"I will teach you." Luca stepped near me, standing a mere inch away from me, his dark eyes piercing into me, the heat of his body radiating in palpable waves. "But you must decide if you want to be with me or not. This is not a proposal of permanence, please know. I am only suggesting we spend more time together. But if you are going to run like a colt every time we experience an intimate moment together, it will not work."

I nodded and opened my mouth to speak, but Luca kept going.

"If you are afraid, only tell me. If you feel you need some time alone to sort out your emotions, tell me. I can give you space to think without you having to go all the way to Paris. I will understand, if you will share your thoughts with me. I promise you this." Luca put his hands on my arms, just below my shoulders. "If you run away again, I will not chase you. I will take it as your choice to not be with me any longer."

"I understand."

He closed the gap between us, our bodies pressed together. His arms wrapped around my waist and his breath was warm on my face, smelling faintly of spearmint. I couldn't believe he'd be able to be with me again, to want me still, after all I'd done to push him away. François's face and fingers rose up in my memory, sending bile into my throat.

I pushed away from Luca.

"What is it?" Luca's eyes narrowed. "There is something, isn't there? You did something, or something happened to you."

I turned away and stared out the window. Paris was slicked with rain and blanketed with gray. Umbrellas bloomed on the sidewalks like geometric flowers, bobbing and nodding with flashes of damp legs and shoes.

"I got drunk the other night. Too drunk. I'm not used to that, you know? I've never really gotten drunk a lot before, so I guess I don't handle it well—"

"What happened?" Luca's voice was tight and hard, prepared for the worst.

"Well this guy started talking to me. I didn't really like him, and I just wanted him to leave me alone, you know? But he was persistent, and—the drunker I got, the more persistent he was. I know now that I should have just left, but then, it didn't occur to me. Well, he kept feeding me drinks, and then I just wasn't able to think straight, and I found myself in a cab with him—"

"Did you sleep with him?"

"I—no, but listen, he—we were in his apartment, and I remember not liking it, and he was touching me, and I didn't like that even more. He was...he was rough. I couldn't get the word out, I was thinking 'no' in my head, as loud as I could, but it wouldn't come out of my mouth. Finally, he touched me down there, and it hurt. That unlocked me somehow—I mean, I could suddenly talk again, and I hit him. I mean, I knocked him straight on his ass and ran out."

"Would you know him again, if you saw him?" Luca asked.

"I suppose—yes, I would. Definitely." I shuddered, his face burned into my mind. "Why?"

"Because we're going to find him and I'm going to shove his head up his asshole."

I shook my head. "No, Luca. Don't. It's not worth it. Besides, it's one man in all of Paris. How are we supposed to find him?"

"You went to his apartment, didn't you? And you came back here from there?"

"Well, yeah, but I don't remember much. I mean, I'm not even sure what bar I was at. I just walked around until I found somewhere kind of busy, and when we left, I was pretty hazy. When I left François's apartment, I just gave the driver the card for the hotel." I turned to Luca and put my forehead to his chest. "I just want to forget him, forget it happened. I want to go back to Italy."

Luca smoothed the hair at the back of my head. His breathing was a loud rush in his chest, his heartbeat a steady rhythm. "Very well, then. Come home with me, and let us start again."

I nodded into his shirt, then looked up at him through my eyelashes. My arms went around his torso, my palms flat on the backs of his shoulders. "Luca? I'm sorry. So sorry. Do you forgive me?"

Luca smiled down at me. His fingers traced the line of my jaw, touched my chin, and then his palms cupped my face. "Of course I do, *mia bella* Delilah. Of course I do. You have been hurt, and betrayed. It is hard to trust again when this has happened. But you must trust me. And when it is impossible to trust, only tell me what you are thinking, and we can find a way past it together, hmmm?"

Our eyes locked, and our lips neared, but he didn't kiss me. I needed, with sudden desperation, to kiss him, to touch him, to feel his hands on me. I needed the physical, tangible reminder of his desire for me.

His love for me. He hadn't spoken the words, but the emotion was there between us, waiting and unspoken. I knew it, he knew it. That, perhaps, was what truly frightened me. It wasn't that I didn't trust Luca; I did. I knew, instinctively and through his constant demonstrations, that he wouldn't hurt me or betray me. I was afraid of his love. I was afraid of needing him. I'd just found my independence, found myself as a woman alone, and suddenly here was a man I wanted, I needed. I loved.

And that, more than anything else, scared the living shit out of me. No matter how far away from him I ran, how I tried to push him away or pretend it wasn't so, I couldn't get away from his presence in my heart, my soul. I couldn't ignore the fact that I wasn't happy away from him.

Even Paris, a place where I think every girl dreams of going, was empty and dull without him.

I felt something crack in my heart, some piece of my resistance breaking off. I leaned up and kissed him, a ferocious slamming of my lips to his, a tiny demonstration of my desperation for him.

He responded exactly as I needed: I felt myself lifted in his impossibly strong arms and carried to the bed. I was wearing yoga pants and a T-shirt, my comfort clothes. He curled his long fingers under the elastic of my pants and panties, stripped them off, then peeled my shirt off, along with the sports bra. In a matter of seconds I was completely nude before him.

I felt a rush of desire pulse through me, soaking the folds of my pussy even before he lowered his mouth to my skin. For a long moment, he merely stood and looked at me, as he had the first time he saw me naked. He had seen me many times since then, but the raw admiration and naked desire for my body hadn't dissipated, hadn't changed. If anything, the knowledge of the pleasure he could find inside me seemed to fan the flames of passion in his eyes even hotter.

I lay on my back on the bed, bare flesh pebbling in the cool air of the hotel room, nipples beading into hard nubs under Luca's fierce gaze. I waited for him, knees up and pressed together, arms crossed over my belly, my gaze heavy-lidded and fixed on his. Luca's lips pressed together and his hands clawed against the dark blue denim of his jeans, his eyes narrowed, his nostrils flared.

I spread my knees apart, just an inch at first, and Luca's fingers knotted in the jeans near his knees. His head tipped back, and he watched me through lowered eyelashes, the tip of his tongue tasting the corner of his mouth and across his lower lip.

My knees split apart even farther now, and the damp petals of my pussy were presented to his gaze. My fingers trailed down my belly, paused on top of my mound, and then drifted down to the crease, paused again at the folds hiding my aching, waiting clit.

My mouth parted and my breath puffed out as I dipped a single finger between my folds to touch the hard, sensitive nub. The pad of my middle finger brushed across my clit, and I couldn't stifle the gasp as it emerged.

That was all it took.

Luca grasped my ankles and drew me effortlessly down the bed so my ass was at the edge, my legs on his shoulders as he knelt down. The collar of his white short-sleeve button-down shirt scraped the soft silk of my inner thighs, and his stubble was like sandpaper against the crease where pussy met thigh. His fingers pulled my lips apart, and his tongue speared inside me to taste the dew of my essence. I heard his breath hiss in delight as he lapped at me. I quivered against him, arching my back. Two fingers slid into my channel, curled upward to find with unerring accuracy the patch of hypersensitive skin and caress it to the rhythm of his questing, circling tongue.

His other hand now slipped up along my side, following the curve of my hip, the padded ridge of my ribs, and cupped my breast, plumped its heavy weight, squeezed the soft globe. I moaned when a rough finger found my nipple and rolled it with exquisite gentility, whimpered when he pinched it.

Colors exploded across my vision; my skin tightened and my muscles trembled. My mouth opened in a silent scream as he licked the juices around my clit, then dragged his tongue across the bead of nerves and made me come, and come, and come again, his fingers inside me, his fingers on my nipple.

I wanted something he'd done before, but I was too shy to say the words. I grabbed the hand playing with my breast and guided it downward, between my legs. I lifted my hips and spread my knees farther apart, pushed his fingers tangled with mine against the rosebud knot of muscle beneath my pussy. Luca didn't hesitate. He dipped his finger inside my folds to lubricate it with my own moisture and then pressed it in tight circles against my anus. I forced myself to relax against the instinctive urge to tighten. His fingers and mouth continued to work my pussy, and I felt another orgasm rising up within me.

His long, slick middle finger worked into me, a slow centimeter at a time. I ground my hips into him, driving him deeper, breathless, coming again.

Every muscle in my body clamped down, and now I was writhing helplessly, pinned in place by his fingers inside me.

"I want you, all of you, now," I gasped.

Luca pulled out of me, leaving me whimpering at the sudden absence. I watched him strip, sat up and reached for him when he was naked, his huge cock standing straight up and straining, the veins visible and throbbing. I wrapped both hands around his girth, and before I even knew what I was planning I had him in my mouth, his satin skin rubbing against my lips. He tasted so good, felt so good, and I sucked on him, glided my hands on him, greedy for him.

He pulled me away from his cock and crawled onto the bed with me. He kissed me, slow and thorough, his tongue tasting of my essence exploring my mouth, his hand roving my body and mine his. We lay down together, bodies twining tangling, tongues touching and tasting, heat merging.

Abruptly, Luca pulled away, a mischievous grin on his lips. He rolled me onto my stomach. Thinking I knew what he wanted, I slid my knees beneath me, presenting my ass to him.

"Take me, Luca," I said. "Take me like this."

He laughed, a low rumble. "Oh, I will. But you know, you were a very bad girl, my Delilah. Very bad, indeed. I think first you must be punished. And this is the perfect position for it."

"Punished?" Fear tinged my voice. What was he going to do?

"Yes. I think you must be spanked."

I panicked. My dad had spanked me as a little girl, under the Biblical principle that sparing the rod spoiled the child. He'd used the dowel from a wooden hanger, a thin rod of wood that stung like a bitch but didn't really leave marks or hurt for more than a few seconds. I know if anyone else was to read this, they'd probably call it child abuse, but it really wasn't. He loved me, and it was his way of guiding me, and I'm none the worse for it, then or now.

But Luca's word, *spanking*, had incited that same sudden spark of fear within me. I moved to roll onto my ass, but Luca held my hips in place.

"What is it? I would not hurt you, you must surely know this. Only a little slap." He tapped one cheek with the palm of his hand, and I relaxed a little. "You were perhaps punished thus as a child? It is not the same. I know, for I was, too. Nowadays, parents are afraid to punish their children, but we survived it, no?"

I held still, afraid to breathe or move, much less speak. I didn't know what I wanted. My arousal had been rather suddenly doused, and part of me wanted to pull Luca close to me and just be held by him. But another part of me knew Luca wouldn't do anything I didn't like, and if I told him I didn't like it, he would stop. And, in truth, the gentle pat of his hand on my bottom *had* felt kind of okay.

It would be fine, right? I kept myself still, fighting the reflex to close up and roll away. Trust took effort, didn't it? Risk and vulnerability weren't things that just happened. You had to make them happen, let them happen. I wasn't a person who found any pleasure in pain, though. But then again, Luca hadn't led me astray so far...

I nodded, a jerky sideways bob of my head as I craned my neck to watch him. He smiled, caressed my spine down from my shoulders to the swell of my tailbone. At first he only rested his hand on the half moon of my right ass cheek, and then he moved his hand in small circles. I felt myself tensing, waiting. His other hand curved up my foot and my calf and my thigh, turning sideways to knife between my legs. His finger brushed my labia, which were dry now. He stroked me with a finger, rubbing the skin of my buttocks with his other. He touched his lips to my hip, then my back, and then, yes, he kissed my ass, a hot, moist caress. I felt my juices begin to flow again, and now his finger delved inside my pussy, just up to one knuckle at first.

I relaxed, realizing he didn't intend to just haul off and start smacking me willy-nilly. I felt silly suddenly for having doubted his ability to give me pleasure, even if I didn't know what I wanted or liked.

I let my hips begin to undulate as he dipped his finger deeper inside me, his other hand moving in broader circles on my ass, alternating between both sides until I was used to his touch there. And then, without warning, he drew his hand back and gave me a resounding slap on the left cheek. My entire backside burst into flames, and I shrieked and jerked forward. The shriek turned into a moan, however, when he thrust his fingers against my clit at the very instant that he slapped my ass, and then he rubbed the spot that he had spanked, smoothing and soothing the reddened skin. He moved to the other side now, circling, small circles, broad circles, his fingers in my pussy again, exploring the walls, brushing my G-spot, not establishing a rhythm but merely touching, keeping me wet and trembling with anticipation.

I was gasping now, waiting for the next slap. When it came, I shrieked again, and once more the sound of protest turned into a drawn-out whimper of pleasure as he pressed the button of my clit in time with the spank. His palm soothed the skin again, then resumed his patternless circling.

The next spank came sooner, and it didn't sting as much, so consumed was I with the rising fires of climax. He had two fingers in my pussy now, swirling around my clit, not quite touching. When he spanked me a third time, he let his fingers brush my clit, almost by accident, and I nearly came. He smoothed the skin, kneeling behind me, one hand between my thighs, the other on my ass, his cock brush against the outside of my leg.

He spanked me again, and this time he smacked both sides in quick succession, the tips of his fingers flicking my clit with each slap. I was moaning nonstop now, and he started to spank me more frequently, one side and then the other, a brush of my nub with each sting of his hand, and now the stinging was changing, spreading a flush throughout me, the slight pain morphing into something else, merging with the fire of orgasm. I rocked my hips back into his hand now, into the fingers on my clit as well as the palm striking my ass.

I came again, ecstasy bursting through me, waves cresting in me with each spank, each circle of my dripping, clenching pussy. I leaned my weight on one forearm and reached behind me with the other hand to grab Luca's cock. I came, and came some more, gasping and shrieking and sliding my hand up and down his length, feeling the slick moisture of pre-come smearing under my palm.

I pulled his cock toward me, drawing him against me, and then he finally pushed his tip between my folds, spearing the flower of my pussy and driving deep inside me. I couldn't stop the scream from escaping, his name leaving my lips as he slid his cock between my tight wet lips, stretching me. He moved slowly, letting me accommodate his size.

His fingers dug into my hips and pulled me back against him. I rolled with his thrust, wanting him deep, wanting to feel him come inside me. He'd given me so much pleasure, and now I wanted to return it. I let my upper torso flatten against the bed, stretching my arms in front of me and keeping my ass raised in the air, impaled by his cock.

He bent over me as he pulled out, and then arched back as he thrust in, his sack slapping against me, his breath grunting out of his lungs, my name a breath of his lips.

He began to move faster now, fluttering his shaft in long quick pulses.

"Come for me, Luca," I said, the words rasping past quivering vocal chords. "Come so hard for me."

"Oh, Delilah," he said, his movements desperate now, his cock pounding into me, "I am...oh, yes..."

"Oh, god, Luca, fuck me harder," I said.

I felt a twinge of surprise at my words, but then the thought was dashed as he began to drive even harder, plunging into me with a primal ferocity. I felt his cock throb and grow thicker, rocked my pussy back down onto him as he stuttered his hips against my ass. He came with a curse, flexing into me, pausing, drawing out, and stabbing deep, a hard thrust against my farthest walls. Hot seed flooded through me, and I felt my inner muscles clench and clamp, felt my belly ripple and my nipples and scalp tighten, my blood boil in my veins and my hand claw into the blanket.

"Yes, yes, don't stop," I said, feeling him still come inside me.

I was just starting to climax again and didn't want him to stop after he'd come. He was still hard inside me, and he began to glide in and out once more, waves of orgasm billowing through me with each pulse of his cock against my walls.

My eyes clamped closed as I came, and now he was driving into me as if he was coming again, but that couldn't be... He seemed as surprised as I was, straightening, gasping. I felt his cock hard and hot inside, throbbing as if full again, but he'd just come. I felt his seed inside me, but he was, he was pounding hard and fast, surprise rife in his ragged moans. He paused long enough to roll me to my back, my pussy rotating around his cock and my leg passing over his head, resting on his shoulder, the other next to his leg.

He wrapped a hand around my thigh and crushed into me, head thrown back and eyes closed. He let go of my legs, and I hooked them around his back, pulled him down to me and kissed him as he came again, shuddering into my aftershocks, his thrusting small, hard, desperate quivers of his hips against mine, so frantic as to be rhythmless.

"*Fottimi...mio dio*...Delilah," Luca whispered, collapsing half on me, half next to me, one leg thrown over mine. "What did you do to me? What was that?"

I could only shake my head and try to calm my breathing. "I don't know. Intense as hell, is what that was."

Exhaustion swept over both of us, and we slept.

I woke disoriented, unsure as to where I was or what had happened, and then I felt Luca's hot, solid bulk next to me, his soft, rhythmic breathing echoing in the darkened hotel room. The drapes were still open, showing the shadows of night-blanketed Paris. I wasn't sure what time Luca had shown up, how long we had made love, how long we had slept.

I slid out of the bed and crept across the room to my netbook, plugged in and sitting open but asleep on the table near the window. I tapped the space bar to wake it up: four-oh-three a.m.

I wrote the preceding entry, letting the emotions of the past five days wash over me and through me.

Now I'm sitting and watching the black fade into gray, bathing Luca's body with dawn light. The sheet covers one leg, revealing his torso, finely muscled and dusted with hair, his limp cock draped over one thigh, his balls sagging to one side. His mouth is slack in sleep, unruly strands of ink-black hair across his forehead and eyes, one hand curled near his face.

I'm struck again, watching him sleep, with the deep, piercing pangs of affection for him, struck again by how beautiful he is, how amazing.

My fingers want to tap out eight letters, a simple declaration of how I feel, but I...I just can't. Not yet.

He's stirring, sensing my absence.

I'm going to save this entry and then crawl back into bed with him, stroke his soft penis until it's hard again. I'm going to slip him inside me as we lie side by side, wake him up with my body flush against his. His hands will wrap around me, his arms cradling me, one hand cupping my breast, the other my mound, his cock inside me, his breath on my neck. He'll begin to move, and he'll moan my name before he's really awake, and then I'll feel his lips curl against the nape of my neck in a smile, and he'll clutch me tighter. He'll move in a purposeful rhythm then, maybe biting my shoulder, fingering my clit and pinching my nipple and thrusting all at once, and we'll come together in the pink and gray of impending dawn, come together in a slow, soul-deep swelling of merged love.

Love.

There's the word I'm so terrified of.

Four of the eight letters: l-o-v-e.

I can write those others, out of order: I; h-i-m.

It's not a puzzle to me. I just can't admit it, even in writing, because I'm too afraid of it being taken away, of it all being a dream, of him changing his mind, of something terrible happening.

Maybe I can try it in Italian: *Io lo amo*.

Oh, god, it's still scary.

No way can I say it to him, in any language. Not yet. If he says it to me, I know I'll freak.

God help me. I don't know if I believe in God anymore, but if you're real and you're out there and you care, God, just...help me through this. Somehow.

He's stirring again. Time to go.

June 22

Good gravy, that didn't go as planned.

He's out getting breakfast for us, so I don't have long.

It started out like I'd thought, as written above. I climbed in bed, took his flaccid cock in my hand and stroked him gently, rubbed my thumb in small circles around the tip. He began to grow under my ministrations, but not quickly enough for my taste, so I scooted down on the bed and got him hard with my mouth. He moaned in his sleep as I licked his crown, massaged his balls until they tightened, grazed him ever so gently with my teeth.

Finally he was fully erect, and I was dripping with anticipation.

I turned my back to his front and guided him in, took his hand in mine and pressed his palm to my heavy breast. I rolled my hips against him and he moved into me instinctively.

I felt him rumble deep in his chest, and his fingers flexed. He stretched, pulling almost out of me, and then arched his back to thrust in.

"Well, a good morning to you," Luca said, a smile in his voice.

"I woke up, and wanted you again, so…"

"You can wake me up like this anytime," he said, squeezing my breast and grinding into me.

We moved together, rolling in tandem, and his arm snaked underneath me to pinch my nipple, his other hand drifting down to cup my mound.

Still all was going according to plan.

Then he reached into the drawer of the bedside table and produced a little bottle of lubricant.

"Where did you get that?" I asked.

"You are not the only one who wakes up in the middle of the night to do mysterious things, you know," Luca said.

"You got up and bought lube?"

"I did not buy it. I brought it with me from home. I simply fetched it from my car."

We were still moving together, but neither of us were near orgasm yet. Luca pulled out of me, slipped his finger down to my ass, and I felt him apply a generous amount of cold, tingling liquid to the tight knot of muscle. I knew this sensation now, and I liked it. I'm not sure what that says about me, and I don't care. It feels good, and he's careful.

His finger slipped in, easier than ever, thanks to the lube. The bulbous tip of his cock was brushing the entrance of my pussy, and I wanted him back inside me, but he wasn't thrusting, and his finger was fully within me, pinning me in place. I could only squirm, impaled by his middle finger.

And then he slipped in another. So, so slowly. Time ceased to pass. All I knew was his fingers inside me, wiggling gently, moving in, stretching me. His other hand circled my waist, hovered on my belly, dipped down to my pussy, slipped in and brushed my clit, pressing it, flicking it, swirled around it.

Juices flowed, fire blossomed, and the not-quite-but-almost painful stretching of his two—three, now?—fingers in my asshole became less painful and more pleasurable. He began to move his fingers in and out, and his hand at my pussy vanished, more lube coated his fingers, and something else, something long and hard yet soft.

I was writhing in helpless abandon. His fingers were inside me, I didn't know how many, couldn't count or feel a difference, just the stretching, stretching, accommodating, filling.

Oh, god, oh, god, just the memory has me quivering, has my asshole quivering as I sit on the bed and type this.

Luca filled me, stimulated me, stretched me, moved in and out of me, and his fingers were in my pussy again, swirling, moving, driving and delving and pushing me closer to orgasm. And now I felt his fingers withdrawing, cold lubricant easing the passage of something huge and hard filling me where his fingers had been.

For the first time in our sexual relationship, I felt fear that I couldn't handle what he giving me. My mouth was wide in a silent scream, and then a soft, barely audible gasp scraped past my clenched throat, and my fingers curled in desperate claws into the bed.

I was still on my side, my knees drawn up, one leg slightly lifted. Luca rolled me in a quick, deft maneuver that had me on my knees with him positioned behind me. I didn't know how much of him I had inside me, but it was enough, almost too much.

"Are you okay, *mia bella*? Is this okay?" Luca's voice was soft, gentle.

I wasn't sure, but I didn't want him out of me. I knew that much, so I nodded, unable to speak. He moved in farther, a slow, careful slide. His fingers were on my hips, more in restraint of himself than an encouragement for me. I felt, through the touch of his hands on my hips, the quivering of his body, the tension of restraint. He wanted to plunge hard, wanted to drive into me, but he wouldn't allow himself.

A little farther then. Oh, god, so full. Again I felt a rush of panic that it would be too much, that I would split in half from his presence inside me. But then he pulled out a little, and the low waves of building climax abruptly peaked as he slid out with excruciating slowness.

I whimpered; Luca growled, tense and trembling. He moved back in, a hesitant, questing thrust, and my entire body convulsed in an orgasm so powerful I felt it in every fiber of my being. I felt it in my teeth, in my scalp, in my fingers and toes and belly and eyes. A scream stuttered out of me, muffled when I buried my face in the bed. Luca growled, a long, low rumble in his chest, and his fingers dug even harder into the crease of my hips as he slid out and plunged back in.

He began to set a rhythm now, slow and steady, and I came with every motion.

But no, this was an orgasm for each thrust; this was merely the buildup.

Oh, god.

When the true climax came, it would shatter me. I knew it in my bones, felt it coming like a freight train.

Luca's sliding cock moved inside me with increasing urgency now, and still with each thrust in, each pull out, I felt a spike of pure intensity, wave after wave building up one atop the other until there was no higher they could go, no more intense they could get.

But they did.

When he'd first begun to move his cock in my tight-clamped channel, I supposed he'd never be able to move freely, that I wouldn't be able to take it like that. But now, somehow, he was pounding into me and I was slamming backward onto him with a ferocity that matched his own, biting the blanket to keep my teeth from cracking in my jaw, my fingers scrabbling at the blankets, my hips moving of their own accord.

I felt his cock burgeon and thicken and pulse, felt his balls tighten as they slapped into my pussy, and then he came with a teeth-grinding roar, slamming into me one, twice, three times; on the third nearly savage plunge, I came.

"Came" doesn't begin to describe it. I'm not sure there are words in any human language for what happened. My universe detonated, shattered, dissolved, imploded. Lights burst behind my eyes, my entire body seized up and convulsed, chemicals rushed through my brain and my boiling blood.

It lasted for an eternity.

I've used the phrase "an agony of ecstasy" before, but in this case, it truly was that. It was something beyond ecstasy that blurred the lines between pleasure and pain.

When it was over, Luca drew out of me, even more slowly than he had pushed in, and I felt my muscles contracting as he withdrew. At last I was left limp and exhausted and shuddering in the blissful haze of aftershocks, some of which were more powerful than some orgasms I've had.

Luca lay down next to me and I turned into him, clutched my arms around his neck and buried my face in his chest. I might have been crying.

"Are you okay?" He must have felt the moisture of my tears against his skin; he sounded worried. "I hurt you?"

I shook my head and tilted my face up to meet his eyes. "No, no. It was...beyond anything... everything..."

"This is good? You are okay?"

"I'm not hurt. It was good. More than good." I kissed his jaw. "It was just so intense. I'm not sure I can handle that very often. It was almost too much, too intense."

Luca nodded his head and smoothed my hair with his hand. "I am not sure I could do that so often, either."

"Why not?" I asked.

"To hold back, so as not to hurt you, but wanting with so much desperateness to just…go so hard in you, it takes much restraint, much controlling of the self. You know? So when I was finally able to release myself, it was all the more intense for having held it back for so long." He kissed my cheek and then my lips. "And you have a way of making nothing of my control. You make me lose my restraint. You are…you so beautiful, so amazing, and I want you so much, all of the time. I just cannot help myself."

Tears pricked my eyes at his words, spoken so casually. I was already emotional from the intensity of our lovemaking, from the volcanic power of my orgasm, and now, such sweet words, said as if it should have been obvious. I couldn't help the sobs.

"Oh, my dear Delilah. Why do you cry?"

I didn't know how to say it, and I was crying too hard to speak. He held me as I wept, didn't ask any more questions, just held me and wiped the tears from my cheeks as they fell.

When I could speak again, I said, "It's just you. The way you treat me, the things you say."

"Is it wrong? The things I say and my treating of you?" Luca sounded confused.

I laughed. "No, no, baby, no. Don't you know women cry from happiness, sometimes?" I sniffed and rubbed my cheek against his stubbly one. "You treat me right. You say things that make me feel... cared for."

"So why does this make you cry? I confess I am puzzled."

"Because no one has ever treated me the way you do. No one has ever said the things to me that you do." I brushed a lock of hair away from his eyes. "It's intense. It's kind of scary. It's a complete change. When you've spent your entire life feeling different, feeling like you're not enough, not good enough, not skinny enough, not pretty enough, it can be really difficult to accept that someone thinks differently, even if it's a good thing."

"Ah, now this I understand." Luca propped himself up on an elbow and caressed my body with his other hand, not a sexual touch, but an affectionate, explorative, tender one. "You do not always see your own worth, I think. You are not so skinny as I think the American ideal of perfection is believed to be."

My brow furrowed and I opened my mouth to speak, but he held up a hand.

"No, please. Only listen. I like you as you are. I say 'like' because I think the other word makes you worried, but it is true enough. I would not like you so much if you were skinny, all sticks and skin. You have curves, you have a body to touch and hold. And also please remember, I am not American. I am Italian, and we have different ideals of beauty. And you, *amore*, are my ideal of beauty."

I melted at that. Who wouldn't? I'm his ideal of beauty? He must see something when he looks at me that I don't.

It occurred to me, as we were drifting off to sleep once more, that I'd called him "baby."

I think I know why people say they're "falling in love."

I've always hated that phrase. I never really understood it. Love was a choice. Something you worked at. I mean, yeah, I understood that you didn't always choose who you fell in love with, that it happened outside of your control. But the verb "to fall"? Why that one? Why falling? It implies a complete loss of control, a total helplessness to stop your tumbling over the edge. When you fall, you transition from solid ground, from balance, into open space, off balance.

When I think "to fall," I think of standing on the edge of a skyscraper. There's no guard rails or Plexiglas walls, just dizzy height, people like ants and cars like toys, the hard ground hundreds of feet below, and you're wavering on the edge, arms flailing, but you can't regain your balance. You're falling. Air rushes past your face in a deafening roar, and you have time to realize, "This is it, I'm going to die."

It's like that with Luca. It's inevitable. I can feel it happening, and I can't stop it. Unlike falling off a building, however, I'm not entirely sure I want to. The loss of control is scary. The vulnerability is frightening.

I wish you could choose to fall in love. Or rather, not fall at all, but walk into love. Live into love. Be in love without falling.

But then, if we didn't fall, implying all the trust and loss of control and complete vulnerability, would it be as sweet? Would it be as satisfying and life-changing? If you could choose it, and control it, would it be as potent and soul-searing?

I think perhaps not, as Luca would say.

June 25

We spent the last couple of days on a Luca-guided tour of Europe. We saw Paris, and it was vibrant and lovely and every bit as romantic as they paint it in the movies. He took me to London and Dublin. We only spent a little time in each place, enough to see the sights and say we'd been there. He also showed me out-of-the-way places, like Belarus, and Ukraine, and Malta. He sold wine, and we made love.

I grew comfortable with him, grew accustomed to his roving, loving gaze on my body as I changed, or showered, or simply lay naked in bed, writing, after we made love. Grew comfortable, but it still never loses its power to stun me.

Like him.

Listen to me, though. Like it's been decades, instead of days.

We're on the way back to Italy now. Italia. Luca is driving, the radio is off, I'm typing with my net-book on my lap ("How can you type on that teeny little thing," Luca asked me, "especially while riding in an auto? It does not give you a headache?" Apparently not.). Luca's hand is on my knee, a familiar touch that makes my heart ache in a sweet and pleasant way.

We're going to be back in Firenze in a couple hours, and I have no idea what will happen when we get there. I'll have explanations to make, I'm sure.

Am I going home? Is Firenze home now? Or my house back in the States? No, I gave that to Harry in the divorce, along with my car, our stocks and the cashed-out value of my 401K, the properties we owned together...everything. So then, would my parents' house be home? No, I haven't lived there since I was nineteen. Certainly not Leah and Mike's house. If they're still together. I'm sure my little shouted tantrum threw some long-held secrets into the light.

So...where is home?

Nowhere.

Firenze?

Whichever hotel I'm in?

Luca's arms.

Shit.

June 27

Luca's grandmother was visiting when we arrived. What a woman. Past eighty, spry and sharp-witted, clear-eyed. A full head of thick black hair liberally streaked with gray, belying her age.

"Luca, where have you been?" she demanded in fluent, accented English as we entered the courtyard. "Why did you leave your poor old grandmother wondering where have you gone? Come, come, my boy. Give your *nonna* a kiss."

Luca grinned at me as he hugged his grandmother and kissed her cheek. "I was on business, *Nonna*. And besides, I did not know you were coming, did I? Am I a mind-reader? I think no. You should call me, if you expect me to be here when you arrive. You know I travel often." He winked at me.

"You should show more respect for your *nonna*, boy. Of course you aren't a mind-reader. Only I am a that. If you were a reader of minds, you would have introduced me to this lovely girl hanging on your arm."

I extended my hand to her. She took my hand as if to shake it, squeezing hard, and pulled me into a hug. "I am *Nonna* Maria." Her eyes were kind, piercing black orbs, truly gimlet in their intensity. "But you will call me *Nonna*, I think. My boy Luca, he is a good boy, no?"

I kissed her cheek as expected. "Yes, he's the best. I'm Delilah."

"Delilah, hmm? It sounds like a flower. You are lovely, like a flower. So much prettier than that sour-faced tart he was married to. *Brutta puttana.*"

"Nonna!" Luca said, shock and something like hurt in his eyes. "Do not talk that way. It is not polite. I know you did not like her, but you should not—"

"Oh, don't you tell me what I shouldn't do, my son. I am eighty-three years old. I have earned the right to speak as I wish."

"You are right, *Nonna*, but at least respect my wishes, and do not speak that way of—"

"Of who? A stupid girl who was never worthy of my favorite grandson? No. She deserves that, and more. *Puttana.* She was never good for you. I said so the very first time I met her. And then she left you, just like that. And stole everything you owned. But I am not supposed to speak ill of her? When she so mistreated you? After all you did for her? Took care of her daughter? Loved her?" *Nonna* Maria shook her finger at Luca. "I will say my mind, and you will listen. Is this girl worthy of you? She is lovely, that much is true. But is she *worthy*?"

Luca took his grandmother's hands in his, met her eyes, and spoke quietly. "She is more than worthy, *Nonna*. She is...everything."

Nonna nodded, her eyes narrow, flicking from me to Luca and back. "And you love her?"

Luca looked from me to his grandmother. He took a deep breath a blew it out slowly. "Yes, I do."

Panic hit me. I couldn't hear anything but the blood pounding in my ears, and that same hot hard something in my gut I felt when I found Harry with Helen. I backed away, but I felt hard fingers around my wrist.

"Look at me, child." *Nonna*'s eyes bored into mine. "Love is not something to fear. Especially not when it is Luca doing the loving. Your fear is misplaced, I think. If you want to love him, you have to wash away the past. Only you can do this, my dear. You must go away, to the sea, perhaps. And you must bathe away all the fears and all the hurts given you by your history."

"*Nonna*, what are you telling her this for? She doesn't need this old woman's folk story nonsense." Luca sounded irritated.

His grandmother swatted him on the back of the head, hard. "Don't be so *sciocco*. It's not folklore, stupid boy. It's the wisdom of an old woman who's had many heartbreaks. I know the look in her eyes. She fears love. She fears hurt." She looked at me, her fingers gentling on my wrist now, hold-ing tenderly rather than restraining. "You don't need a hot springs, or a special place, or any fancy prayer. You only need the time alone, to decide truly what you want. If you want to run away at only the word 'love,' then you have deeper fears. I know this. I have had these fears. His grandfather was not the first man I loved, but he was the last, and it was very hard for me to learn to love him. My story is one for another time, perhaps. But you cannot think to go further into love if you do not trust yourself to know what you want. And you do *not* know."

"*Nonna*, you—"

"Luca, no. She's right," I interrupted. "You know she is."

Luca nodded. "I know, I know, but we just... you—"

"It'll be fine, Luca." I put my hand on his arm. "I'm not running, I promise."

"And you're not going anywhere yet," Luca's mother, Domenica, said, emerging from the kitchen. "It is time for dinner. The rest will soon be here, I think. They will all want to see you."

She hugged me, as if I was her daughter. This simple act of familiarity had my eyes burning and my throat thickening. My own mother had stopped hugging me when I became a teenager. When we saw each other as adults, it was an awkward, back-patting, several-feet-of-space-between-us kind of hug. But this hug from Domenica was a completely different thing. It was warm, safe, familiar, as if she'd always hugged me. It would be overly dramatic and not precisely true to say that all my worries and fears evaporated when she hugged me, but I did feel a lot better.

Luca took my hand and led me into the kitchen, which now felt more like home than my own ever had. I sat at the huge block of age-polished wood that was the kitchen table and chatted with *Nonna*, Domenica, and Luca while coffee percolated on the stove. I heard voices in the courtyard, Elisabetta and Lucia, Luca's sisters—with their husbands Fillipo and Claudio. Behind them came Giuliana and Marta, his sisters-in-law, with their husbands—Luca's brothers—Lorenzo and Niccolò. Woven around the adults' chatter was the babble and laughter of children, eleven of them between the four couples.

I felt a moment of panic at all the voices, all the people and personalities, all the names to keep straight. This one family, without even any of the aunts and uncles from Domenica's and Dante's sides of the families, represented more people than I knew back in the States. I knew people, so that might not have been a totally true statement. It would be more accurate perhaps to say I was acquainted with most of the town, knew most people by face and name. But Luca's family, these were people I'd spent time with. I knew more than their names and faces. I'd broken bread and drank wine with them, dandled babies and done dishes with them. If things went further with Luca, they would be…family.

Panic boiled even hotter, igniting my flight reflex: *run, run, run*.

Luca's hands descended on my shoulders, massaging gently. His whiskers brushed my ear, and his voice rasped gently: "Relax, *amore*. Do not be worried. It will be fine. Only breathe, and be calm."

I wondered how he knew what I was thinking. Did my panic show on my face? I turned my face to his, our lips brushing. He kissed me, a light, quick peck meant to reassure.

"How'd you know?" I asked.

Luca laughed and pointed at my hands: I'd picked up a fork and bent it nearly in half. I let go of the fork and it clattered to the table, my fingers suddenly throbbing. Luca straightened it effortlessly and took my hand in his, threading our fingers together.

Lucia was the first to enter the kitchen, a little boy about two years old on her hip. "Delilah, you have returned!" She set the little boy on his feet, and he immediately toddled over to Domenica and tugged on her apron to be picked up. "You left so suddenly, we were all worried for you."

Luca frowned at his sister, shaking his head imperceptibly. I squeezed his hand. "I know I did, Lucia, and I apologize for making you all worry. I'm just—I have issues sometimes. Nothing to worry about."

Lucia took the percolator from the stove, grabbed half a dozen mugs from a cabinet by their handles, and poured coffee for everyone before resetting the percolator with fresh grounds and water. This family drank coffee at all hours, it seemed.

Lucia took a seat by me on the opposite side from Luca. "You know, I think if we are going to be sisters, you should be truthful with me."

"Lucia," Luca said, "do not be so—"

"It's fine, Luca," I interrupted. "She's right."

Luca muttered something in Italian about always being interrupted by women, but held his silence.

"The truth is, I'm not sure what's going on with Luca and me. Things are complicated."

"Complicatedness is a part of living, I think," Lucia said, and sipped her coffee. "It is no reason to run away from a man who loves you."

I suppressed a bolt of irritation. Lucia was right, as the women in Luca's family so often seemed to be.

"You don't know my complications, Lucia," I said, trying to keep my voice even. "I can't just..." I trailed off, unsure what I couldn't just do.

Lucia waved her mug at me, a dismissal. "Bah. I do not think it is so complicated as you would like to make it. Fear and complicatedness are not the same thing, you know." She leaned forward and put her hand over mine. "I like you, so I will speak *francamente*. I think you are not so complicated, not having so many issues as you intend us to think. You are only afraid of committing, for having been betrayed in your history. This I understand, and am not meaning to make little of your fears. But you must be brave, if you wish to defeat your fears and have a happy life with a man who loves you. Which would be Luca, in case I am not being *chiaro*."

I nodded. "I think you're right. But…it's not as to do as it is to say."

"True, it is true. I did not say it was easy, only right." Lucia seemed satisfied with having said her piece. She plucked her son from his grandmother and set him down to walk. "If he is always held, Mamma, he will not ever learn to be able to walk as a big boy."

Domenica responded in Italian, too fast for me to follow, but it was something about a grandmother's right to spoil her grandchildren, I think. Lucia just rolled her eyes and followed her son into the courtyard, where the laughter of children echoed, a joyous, exuberant chorus.

Dinner was a raucous affair, lasting well into the night. Children fell asleep in their parents' arms and were laid down in available beds while the adults continued to drink and talk.

The last time I remember looking at a clock, it was two in the morning and I was thoroughly and pleasantly drunk on excellent wine. I felt safe, though, protected and comfortable. I could be myself, I didn't have to worry about getting back to a hotel, or being taken advantage of, or judged.

Luca led me upstairs to the same bedroom we'd been in before, overlooking the courtyard. I stumbled up the stairs, held steady by Luca's strong hands, felt myself lifted into bed, wine-breath on my face as he leaned in for a kiss. His lips met mine, and he wobbled above me, making me realize he was as drunk as I was. I smiled into the kiss, scratched at his waist for the bottom edge of his shirt, and lifted it off.

We fumbled at each other's clothes, laughing at how clumsy we were, missing buttons, falling over as we tried to lift up to get our pants down past our hips. Luca struggled for a pathetically long time with the hooks of my bra, eventually giving up and falling over.

"I cannot do it, *amore*," he said, sloppily kissing my spine. "I cannot make out how many hooks and hoops are there."

I managed to get the bra off, and then we were both naked. Luca pulled the chain to turn the light off, and then we were lit only by the silver wash of the full moon shining in through the open window.

Luca and I lay side by side on the bed, facing each other. His hand rested on my waist, just above the swell of my hip. His lips touched my shoulder, and then my arm near my elbow. He wound our fingers together and lifted my arm over my head, lowering his mouth to the mound of my breast, nipping the taut bud of my nipple. I whispered Luca's name, rolled to my back and feathered my fingers through his hair as he paid homage to one breast and then the other.

I felt his finger dip past my navel to trace the crease of my labia. "Yes, Luca, touch me," I said, spreading my legs apart.

He smiled against my nipple and slipped the finger into the wet, tight, heat of my pussy. I arched my back, eyes closed, and exulted in his touch. I reached between our bodies and wrapped my fingers around the hot, hard silk of Luca's cock, heard his moan against my skin as I moved my hand on his length.

I pushed Luca's shoulder to roll him onto his back and slid down his body, resting my cheek on his belly. I took him in my mouth, not touching him with my hands at first, just my lips and tongue on his salty, soft skin.

The world spun around me, the bed undulated, and I closed my eyes to block it all out, focused on the taste of his skin, the tang of his leaking pre-come, his huge shaft thick and throbbing in my hands, the heat of his body against my face. I felt myself lifted and moved, and then Luca's stubble brushed my thigh. I was on my side, Luca's cock in my mouth and my hands, and then I felt my leg pushed up and rested on firm, solid flesh, and then something warm and wet speared into my pussy. He was licking me as I sucked him.

Oh, god. Good gravy. There was a term for this, something odd, two numbers, but I couldn't remember it, and it didn't matter then. All I knew was that it felt incredible. The angles were a bit awkward, but I didn't care. He was in my mouth and he was in my pussy all at once; we were a never-ending cycle of pleasure. My lit-major brain floated a word to me: *ouroboros*, a serpent or dragon eating its own tail, a symbol of eternity, or self-reflexivity.

Apparently my drunken mind couldn't come up with the term "sixty-nine," but it could remember the definition of *ouroboros*.

That was us, self-perpetuating pleasure, cyclical love. We broke apart at the same moment, and I climbed up Luca's prone body, rested my weight on his chest and my forearms. My hips lifted and I impaled myself on him, slid him in to the hilt in one smooth motion. There was no gradual immersion this time, just full, deep, immediate penetration, sweet surrender to his body's fit with mine.

His hands pulled my hips onto his, lifted and pulled, and his mouth found mine as we dove into climax together. There was no moaning or screaming this time. Only whispers and sighs, names uttered in the moment of ecstatic release.

I don't remember falling asleep. I woke up tangled with him, sticky and smeared and sated, head aching with the sharp slice of a wine hangover, sunlight streaming in through the window.

I've started the habit of leaving my netbook on the bedside near me when I sleep, or on the floor, somewhere close at hand so I can write as soon as I wake up, put down on screen the previous day's memories while they're fresh upon waking.

Luca is stirring, and it's time for some morning lovin', and then a shower, and then coffee.

I'm almost ready to say it. His family is right; my fear is all that's holding me back. But then, my fear is a potent thing. When I think of saying "I love you," I think of Harry, of saying those words to him every day for over a decade, rarely hearing him say it back, rarely—if ever—seeing it in action. Knowing, in a swift and sudden and gut-wrenching revelation, that he never did love me.

Luca is awake, watching me type with sleep-blurred eyes, blanket rucked around his hips, one arm beneath his head, a half-smile on his lips.

"Put that away and come here to me," he is saying.

I'm continuing to type as he reaches for me, just to irritate him. Oh, god, he's not playing fair, touching my pussy as I type. This is fun...I can't concentrate, can't think, and now,

oh the hell with this game I'll finish the entry later

June 28

I decided to leave the previous entry's ending the way it is. It's cute, I think.

I'm sitting on a beach on the west coast of Italy. I don't know the name of the quaint little town with the picturesque ruins on the bluff and the stone buildings that have known the chatter of villagers since before America saw the trod of European feet.

I took a train here to get some time to think and make some clear-headed decisions.

It's too easy to think with my body and my heart when I'm with him. My mind and my logic get pushed aside, and if I'm going to make a rational decision, I need to get away from the potent, heady drug that is Luca.

But he isn't a drug, is he? He doesn't alter my mind, or change me. He turns me into who I truly am. I'm carefree with him, unfettered and liberated and full of life. His family is so loving, so generous, so welcoming, that I feel them to be more truly my family than my own blood back in the States.

My father is cold and judgmental, quick to hand down ultimatums and hard-nosed demands, slow to affection, spare with praise and compliments. Mother is the same, but more passive-aggressive, willing to wait and watch and gather evidence against you, and then strike when the moment is right. She's tactical.

Leah is Miss Perfect. Straight As, effortlessly. Captain of the cheer squad, debate team, vice president of the student council three years in a row, popular, fun, skinny. Married a stable, caring man after a short engagement, had kids, got a house with an actual, factual white picket fucking fence. Pretended life was spiffy and perfect, like she always has. And then she fucks my husband.

Not that I'm bitter.

I can't see Elisabetta sleeping with Lucia's husband. It just wouldn't happen. Not ever.

It's funny, I can barely remember the States. I'm speaking in Italian more and more. It hasn't shown through in this diary, I'm realizing, since I've stopped transcribing the Italian, except where it pops up when someone is speaking English. I had a dream in Italian. I called out Luca's named during sex, and instead of "yes, yes, yes," I said "*si, si, si.*"

Even now I'm thinking I'm ready to go home, and the image that pops into my head is the house in Firenze, filled with light and laughter and love. And Luca. I can see myself in Firenze, in a little flat not far from Domenica and Dante's house. There would be flowers in a planter on the window, wash hanging to dry in the age-old way, a checked table-cloth on a round table in the kitchen, a candle made from an old wine bottle.

There might even someday be a little boy or girl running about the flat, ink-black hair and dusky skin and cerulean eyes.

The sun is setting, shedding fiery orange light onto the rippling azure field of the ocean. Gulls caw, children splash in the surf a hundred feet down the shore. A sail blinks white on the horizon.

So, the decision.

Am I afraid of loving Luca? Yes. *Hell*, yes. I'm afraid it'll end up like things with Harry did, and I'll be stuck here in Italy, an ex-pat with no money left and no ties to anywhere, old and alone and too tired to start over again.

I'm afraid of being hurt again, betrayed again. I'm afraid of having a child with him, because that will mean I'm permanently tied to him, and if it ends, if he cheats, or doesn't actually love me till death do us part, then I'll be well and truly fucked.

But I know, in my heart as well as in my mind, that he does love me like that. I know it on a vis-ceral level. He came to Paris at a single phone call, even after I'd ran away from him not once, but twice. He's shown me the wonders of sex. He shows me, each and every day, that I am beautiful and worthy of love.

He calls me "*amore*." His love. He looks at me with adoration shining in his coal-black eyes. He touches me as if I was a work of art, a sculpture crafted by God for Luca and Luca alone.

I was.

He makes me almost believe in God again, even though I stopped a long time ago.

He loves me.

And I love him.

June 29

I'm writing this from the swaying silence of a sleeper car in a train. Another train. This one is en route from Firenze to a winery in Tuscany. Why am I going to Tuscany? To find Luca.

He didn't exactly run away, like I did on him, but he left rather abruptly.

I got off the train in Firenze, practically ran to his parents' house to find him and tell him my news. I burst through the door into the courtyard, shouting his name. The courtyard was empty, silent.

I stopped in my tracks, confused. He'd said he'd be here when I got back, waiting for him. I called him from the hotel before I left the coast, telling him when my train would arrive.

So where was he?

I went into the kitchen, found Domenica sitting at the table drinking coffee and playing solitaire. I poured myself a mug of coffee, doctored it to my liking, and sat down with a huff. My breath knocked some of Domenica's cards out of alignment, and she shot me an irritated glance, then noticed the distress evident on my face.

"He had to work, child. It was some kind of emergency at one of the...*cantine*, oh, *madre di dio*, what's the word—winers? No. Wine-making places. I cannot think of the word in English. But that is where he went. To Montepulciano. He will be back in a few days, he says."

"Wineries," I said.

"Yes, that is it. Thank you. So, please. Do not worrying. Only relax and have more coffee. Help me cook a dinner. Play me in some cards. He will be back before you know it."

I shook my head. "No, Domenica. I can't wait. I have to talk to him."

"Oh?" Domenica didn't look up from her cards, but I could sense her curiosity burning.

I decided to reply in Italian, for some reason. "*Io lo amo.*"

"I know this, *figlia*," she said. "And so does he."

Figlia. Daughter. My eyes burned at the casual way she said the word.

"Well, I didn't. And he hasn't heard me say it. I need to see him."

Domenica looked up from the cards, smiled at me. She left the table and went to a drawer in a corner of the kitchen, one full of random items, the ubiquitous junk drawer. She rummaged until she found an envelope full of brochures, flipped through them until she found the one she was looking for.

"I believe it is this one he went to. If not, they should be able to locate him for you." Domenica handed me the brightly colored, trifold sheet of glossy paper, printed in Italian. I found the address on the back, copied it down, thanked Domenica. I exchanged the clothes in my overnight bag for clean ones and headed straight back to the train station, acquired a ticket that would take me part of the way.

Now I'm nearly there, the train is pulling into the station. My heart is already in knots and butterflies, even though I know I still have to find the winery, and he may not be there.

It's four in the morning, and I can't sleep. My head's all awhirl, as my grandfather used to say.

As I write, my fingers tremble, my gut churns, and my heart pitter-patters.

I said yes.

Argh. Go back, Delilah. Tell the story from the beginning. Telling the story makes it real, helps me tamp down the nerves and deal with the emotions.

Luca snores next to me. Even now, asleep, he rolls over, and his hand stretches across my lap to hug my hip. I can't help smiling at the peace in his features, the happiness.

That makes it all all right.

Go back to the beginning.

I stepped off the train, bag over my arm, sunglasses on against the brilliance of the Tuscan sun. I asked the teller at the station window how to get to the winery, and he suggested renting a car, gave me directions to the rental place just down the street.

I got there, and they had no cars. Well, none that I could drive. See, I can't drive a stick shift, and all the cars were manual transmissions. So I ended up renting a Vespa, a little moped scooter thing. It was baby blue and nearly as old as I was, but it ran. I only had one bag, which I strapped to the seat behind me with fraying bungee cords lent to me by the rental agent, who also gave me further directions.

What no one told me was how far away from the main village the winery itself was. Maybe it wasn't that far. Maybe it was just my nerves combined with the turtle-like top speed of the Vespa, which wasn't much faster than I could've walked, honestly. Either way, it seemed to take forever.

It was beyond beautiful. Quintessential Italy. Picturesque rolling hills, row after orderly row of grapevines vanishing over the horizon. Bright sun, blue sky, puffs of cotton clouds. Hot, but not stifling.

I found the main building of the winery after over an hour of tootling along winding roads on an aged scooter. An older man found me wandering along a rack of dusty wine bottles, labeled and unlabeled.

"Can I help you?" he asked in slow Italian.

"Yes," I said, in a more normally paced conversational tone. "I'm looking for Luca. I was told he might be here."

"Luca?" The old man wrinkled his brow and rubbed a gnarled finger along his upper lip. "Oh, yes, yes. Luca. He is here, somewhere. Out in the grapes, I think. That way."

He pointed at the rolling hills, a vague wave of his hand. "You could wait for him here. It might be easier, you know. The fields are vast. He could be anywhere."

"What is he doing?" I asked.

"Doing? Oh, I have no idea, I am sure. Something important. He is part owner, after all."

"Owner? I didn't know he owned the winery."

The old man shrugged. "Not fully. It's a new thing. There was some problem with the grapes, or an account, perhaps. I don't know. Wait here, if you wish. I can pour you some wine. Or you can go look. Leave your bag here. It will be safe. I'm the only one around."

"I'll go look," I said, setting my bag on a counter.

The old man shrugged, took the bag, and set it behind a counter out of sight, then waved to me and tottered off.

I set out into the fields. They stretched in every direction, quickly confusing my sense of orientation. I walked for maybe ten minutes, birds wheeling above me, their twittering the only sound besides the wind.

And then I heard his voice. I found him examining a section of vines that seemed to have been eaten by a bug of some sort. He was talking to another man a few years older than he in rapid-fire Italian. I watched from a few feet away, as the two seemed to be arguing rather vehemently, and I didn't want to interrupt.

A dog barked behind me, startling me. Dogs don't exactly scare me, but I don't like them. I shrieked and jumped about a foot in the air, turning to see a dog the size of a small horse standing behind me, tongue lolling out of its mouth. It had huge dagger-like teeth, paws as wide as dinner plates, with things that looked suspiciously like swords in place of claws. The dog/horse/dragon trotted a few steps closer to me, sniffed my feet, my knees, and then my crotch. I squealed and stumbled backward away from the dog, who followed me and sat on my feet. It then barked, a sound loud enough to deafen me, showing me a mouth full of teeth and a long, pink tongue. Sure, it looked like it was smiling with its tongue flopped out like that, huffing its nasty breath on my chest. Yeah, it was tall enough sitting down that its head was near my tits.

"Get away," I said in English.

The dog didn't move. I heard muffled chuckles behind me, but I didn't dare take my eyes off the massive, flesh-eating beast in front of me. Then I remembered I was in Italy, and the dog wouldn't be trained to obey English commands, but Italian. That's not something I'd ever thought of before then.

"Scendere me, cane! Scendere!"

The dog just barked. My feet were going numb from the two or three tons of dog flesh sitting on them. I gathered my courage and pushed on its chest, but it didn't move. It was like trying to push a building. It nudged me with its nose, and I fell over backward, my feet pinned by its huge backside. It was probably smearing dog shit on my feet, unless it had used its tongue, which had started licking my face, to clean it all off.

I don't like dogs.

Luca's voice washed over me. "Brutus, *vieni qui.*"

The dog, Brutus, barked in my face, spatter-
ing me with slobber, and then loped away to sit by
Luca. I sat up, wiped my now slobber-sticky face,
and struggled to my feet.

Luca was unsuccessfully trying to smother a
smile. "Delilah, *amore*, what a pleasing surprise to
see you here!"

He came over to me, lifted the bottom edge of
his T-shirt, and wiped my face clean with it. I pulled
a travel-size bottle of sanitizer from my purse and
smeared it on my face and hands, to the uproarious
laughter of Luca and the other man. The dog had
left Luca's side to sit on the other man's feet, and
the man was scratching Brutus' ear absently.

"Well, you were gone when I got back, and I
had to see you. I wasn't sure when you'd be back,
and your mom told me you'd be here, so I came. I
hope I'm not interrupting anything."

Luca waved his hand in a dismissal. "No,
no. Just a little thing with the grapes. Some kind
of insect was eating the crop. We will fix it, no
problems."

"I didn't know you were part owner," I said.

Luca shrugged. "It is not so big of a thing. I
work for Giancarlo and Mario for many years.
When Mario retired, he sold me part of his share
for discount."

The other man, who I assumed was Giancarlo,
waved at Luca and set out through the rows of

grape trellises, Brutus at his heels. When he was out of sight, Luca wrapped me in an embrace.

"You came all the way here only to talk to me?" Luca asked.

I nodded, staring up at him, my arms wrapping around his waist. "I came all the way here to say three words: I love you."

Luca smiled and kissed me, a slow, heated possession of my lips. "You had good thoughts at the coast, then?"

I toyed with the top button of his shirt, and it somehow came undone. "It's not so complicated after all. I belong here, with you."

Three more buttons had come undone while I spoke, and then his shirt was off, tumbling in the light breeze to the dirt underfoot. Luca's fingers skimmed my skin between shorts and shirt, then lifted my shirt over my head. He made quick work of the front clasp to my bra, and then I was topless among the vines, the hot Italian sun shining on us.

"Will what's-his-name come back?" I asked as I unzipped and unbuttoned Luca's jeans.

"Giancarlo? No. He was going home, he said. No one will come out to this section of the fields again." Luca stood naked in the sunlight, and my blood raced at the sight of him.

It never failed. His beauty always stunned me, the toned perfection of his muscles, the hard angles and thick slabs of male strength. My shorts fell away, and then Luca spread our clothes on the dirt, lay down on top of them, and drew me down to him. He was soft beneath me, somehow, despite the hardness of his body. Our lips met, fire lighting in my belly and spreading down to pool between my thighs.

We'd been together many times since I'd arrived in Italy. In beds, on the ground outside, various positions…but this was different. I'd finally broken through the final layer of resistance to the feelings between us. This wasn't just an education in the delights of sex anymore. It never had been. This was love. This was an expression of our feelings for each other, our desire to get closer to one another.

The term "making love" is so often used you don't stop to think about it. But it really is an apt term for what sex truly is between two people who love each other. You are bare, body to body. It's complete vulnerability, physically. Every flaw of your body is on display. If you're in a relationship where you're open and trusting of your partner, then you're totally vulnerable with them emotionally as well. That takes bravery. If you think about it, making love, having sex, is an act of incredible trust. You are placing your body at the mercy of the other person. Your performance, your abilities and experience or lack thereof, is presented for inspection. All you are, as a person, is there to be seen.

With Luca, I realized—or I'm realizing now as I write this—that it had always been a physical relationship for me. I enjoyed the things he made me feel. I enjoyed his touch, the sight of his body, the unbelievable bliss of orgasm. But I don't think I truly appreciated the gift Luca was giving me until that afternoon in the grape fields of Montepulciano. He was giving me himself. He was trusting me with his emotions. It was never just sex for him. He was taking a risk, a huge risk that almost didn't pay off. If I hadn't been able to face the truth of my love for him, he would have been heartbroken.

I saw this in his eyes as he cradled me against him, there in the dirt with the smell of soil and sun on foliage. Our bodies merged in a dance of union. It wasn't mere penetration—it was beyond terms like "cock" and "pussy." I've used those terms, and I will again, because I like them. They're dirty and raw and honest. But there was more, in that moment.

I struggle, even now, to contain and fathom the enormity of true love made physical expression. It seems a fairy-tale thing, those words: true love. It's something for the storybooks. For the prince and his lady as they kiss against the sunset after defeating evil. It's something every girl dreams of, playing Barbies and House and watching the chick-flick romance movies.

And I almost missed it.

He held me to his chest and kissed my lips with tender passion as he moved into me. His body was the softest, most comfortable bed, his arms wrapping me in a protective cocoon, his hands caressing my skin, his hardness sliding inside my slick heat, driving the fires hotter, pushing my love for him deeper with every stroke.

Our kiss broke and our eyes met as we moved. I opened myself, heart, mind, body, and soul, to what he was offering. I let the fears slide away, beading as sweat on my skin. He saw me, truly saw me, and he loved me, for all I was. I tried to take it in, to get my heart around it, to get my soul to grasp it, my mind to understand it, but I couldn't. It was too much.

I smiled from pure joy as tears streamed down my face. I kissed him, salty wetness mingling as our lips touched, and he didn't ask what was wrong. He saw the overwhelming flood tide of emotions coursing in me, and he accepted it, radiated it back.

He moved, he caressed, he slid and slipped and touched and kissed. He loved. Slowly, furiously, perfectly. He filled me, set me alight.

I'll let one cliché slide: He completed me. Clichés are so often repeated because of their inherent truth. In this, the truth is undeniable. The person who truly, madly, deeply loves you does in fact complete you. The Bible speaks in Genesis about man cleaving to the woman, and they become one flesh. Even if you don't read the Bible, you've heard the phrase bandied about, most likely. Well, that's another phrase that has deep meaning if you stop to think about it.

One flesh. It's more than a joining. More than a physical meeting of bodies. You truly merge, especially in the instant of mutual climax. Space and time and boundaries between identities fade away, until all that exists for those brief, endless seconds is you, one melded person, one self. You. One you, from two fragments of I.

We became one flesh. I stopped worrying about the future, about the past, about what if. I let my love well up and burgeon, become larger, swell and sway and ignite and catalyze. His body moved within mine, and passions flared until passion drifted away and became something else. I breathed in his scent, felt the heat of his skin against mine and his lips on my flesh and his hands on my back and buttocks and in my hair.

Climax came as a sobbing eruption of raw emotion. His fingers coiled in my hair and he breathed my name, a prayer to the winds. He moved with desperation, writhing beneath me as if there was no way to get close enough.

"I love you, Luca," I gasped.

Our eyes met, burned, wavered with tears.

"*Ti amo*, Delilah. I love you," Luca whispered, thrusting with each syllable. "*Ti amo. Ti amo.*"

We went still and silent, eventually.

I put a scene break here simply because I wanted to place some space between the majesty of that experience and all that came after.

We dressed and made our way through the fields back to where I'd parked. Luca had a good laugh at the Vespa I'd ridden to get to the winery and told me he knew the rental agent, that he'd arrange to have it picked up for me. We fetched my bag from inside the building, and Luca led me around back to where he'd parked.

He drove us back to Montepulciano, to a little inn where he'd let a room for the night. We showered, made love again in the shower. Oh, lord, how amazing. Hot water sluicing down on our bodies, washing away the dirt of travel and relaxing our muscles, pleasure rippling through us, heat in us and on us and around us. He pinned me against the wall and held my leg up around his waist, plunged up into me, lifting onto his toes as he thrust. I bit his shoulder with each hard thrust, moaning into the firm silk of his flesh, tasting skin and water. I moaned his name in his ear as I came, and then he shot his hot seed into me, his lips meeting mine with each thrust of his release.

And then we had to wash all over again. The water ran lukewarm by the time we were clean and dry. We dressed, and Luca led me out onto the streets, bustling with tourists and locals, splashing fountains lit yellow in the dark of descending night. We found a table at a little restaurant and talked over wine, pasta, and cannolis.

I was learning more and more Italian with every passing day, and larger portions of our conversations were taking place in Luca's language rather than mine. This seemed fitting. I was learning to express myself, and he would gently correct my grammar or pronunciation or syntax.

We left the little cafe and strolled the streets, hand in hand, sometimes talking, sometimes not. And then we turned a corner and Luca froze, his hand crushing mine with sudden strength.

A woman stood in front of us, holding a young girl of maybe ten years by the hand. I knew instinctively who this was: Lia and Luisa.

Two gut reactions warred within me. One part of me wanted to drop Luca's hand; the other part wanted to lean closer, wrap my arm around his waist, and establish my claim.

Lia's eyes widened with surprise and then wavered with fear. Luisa seemed confused, as if she didn't know what she felt.

No one spoke for a long tense moment.

"Lia…" Luca said in Italian. "I did not expect to see you here."

"We are just passing through," Lia responded, after a brief pause. "We were visiting family in the north."

Luca licked his lips, and his hand flexed in mine. I held still, not letting go or moving closer to him.

"Luisa," Luca said. "You have grown tall. How are you?"

Luisa looked first to her mother and then back at Luca. "I am a child. Children grow." She tilted her head to the side. "Why did we suddenly no longer live with you, Luca? Mamma won't speak of it."

Luca's face contorted as he struggled to find an answer, and to contain his emotions. "It…that is a hard question to answer, Luisa." He knelt down, and I rested my hand on his shoulder; I knew, on some bone-deep level, that he needed the constant contact with me to get through this sudden, sur- prising meeting. "It is something that is difficult for even adults to talk about, sometimes."

Luisa frowned. "What you mean to say is that you will not tell me, because I am a child. 'You won't understand, Luisa.'" She spoke as if by rote, in a deep voice. "'I will explain when you're older.'"

Luca rubbed his face with his hand. "You are a smart young lady, so I will not tell you any lies, or any such nonsense as that. I do not know why your mother did not want to live with me anymore. I am sure she had her reasons, though, and I know she loves you, and wants the best for you."

"Well, yes, I know that. She is my mother. Mammas love their daughters. But I have wondered for a very long time why we left. I thought maybe it was because you did not want to be a papa to a girl who was not your own."

Lia choked back some kind of outburst. Luca glanced up at her briefly and then back to Luisa. He put his hand on the girl's arm.

"No, little one. That is not the reason. I would—" He cut himself off. "No. That is not the reason. You must know that. Okay? It was not anything that you did do, or did not do. It was not you."

Luisa nodded. "Mommy has a boyfriend, you know. His name is Marco. He is nice, but he is not so handsome as you, I think." She seemed to have accepted his answer in the way of children, and then moved on.

"Luisa, that is enough," Lia cut in, flushing. She tugged Luisa's hand. "We should go. Say good-bye, Luisa."

Luca stood up. He glanced at me, and in that brief meeting of our eyes, I saw a welter of emotions. He looked at Lia again, opened his mouth to speak, and then closed it again with a glance back at me.

I thought I understood what he was debating. "Ask her, Luca," I said in English.

He nodded and squeezed my hand. "Why *did* you leave, Lia? I need to know. It will not change anything, nor do I wish to. But...I need to know."

She shook her head, glanced down at Luisa and back to Luca. "You were not right for me. You wanted something from me I could not give, and I did not know how to say it. So I left."

Luca shook his head. "That is not it. You took everything, Lia. *Everything*."

"I had no job, no skills. I did not know how I was going to support us, Luisa and I, when I left. I know it was wrong, and I am so very sorry. I have regretted it, since. You are a good man, and you deserved better treatment than that." She looked at her feet. "You deserved better than me."

"If you had just told me—" Luca began.

"No more, Luca," Lia cut in. "Not here, not now. I have given you an explanation. It is enough."

I felt a rush of the old panic at the raw emotion evident in Luca. I'd thought he was over it, past it, but now, with this, I suddenly wasn't so sure.

Lia tugged Luisa into a walk, moving past us. "Goodbye, Luca. I hope you have a happy life. I hope you have found what you deserve."

Luisa pulled free of her mother and hugged Luca. "Will I see you again?"

Luca shook his head slowly. "No, Luisa. You will not."

She nodded. "Maybe I will find you when I am older, and we can be friends."

"Perhaps we can," Luca said. He gave her gentle nudge toward her mother. "Now you should go. You must not keep your mother waiting. She does not like to be late."

Luisa and Lia rounded the corner out of view. Luisa looked back one last time as she disappeared.

Luca was quiet for a long time, staring after them, as if he could see them walking away.

"Are you okay?" I asked.

Luca nodded. "It was a shock to see them, after all this time."

He pulled on my hand, and we resumed walking. After a few steps I had to ask.

"Are you over her? For real?"

Luca looked at me, frowning. "Over her? Of course I am over her. As I said, it was a great shock to meet them so unexpectedly."

I shrugged. "I don't know. You just seemed upset. I thought maybe you were...missing her."

Luca shook his head. "Upset, yes. The way she left me hurt me very much. It is why you running away as you did was so difficult for me. Why I could not move on if you did it again. I was upset, yes...but miss her? No. We were not right for each other. She was correct in what she said. She could not give me what I needed, nor I could I give to her what she needed, it seemed. She took the cowardly way out, but it is over. It is done. I was more upset for the sake of Luisa. I always hoped she did not think I abandoned her. I feel better, now, after speaking to her. She knows I did not abandon her. It all I could ask for, from that situation."

I felt better then. "As long as you're sure you don't—"

He stopped, pushed me back against the wall, and interrupted me with a kiss. "Only you, *amore*. Only you, my Delilah. I want her no more than you want Harry back. It is done, for the better of both of us."

We kissed in the orange glow of a streetlight, the soft plash of a fountain the soundtrack of our lips' dance. We walked the streets of Montepulciano for a while longer after that. We returned to our room in the wee hours, and made love yet again.

Each time is different. In the grape fields it was slow and languorous and deeply emotional; in the shower it was rough and hungry; then, late at night, in the darkness of the room lit only by stars and city lights, it was wild and noisy and acrobatic, exhausting and satiating.

I lay in his arms, panting, sweat-slick, quivering from aftershocks and afterglow.

Luca's fingers were toying with my hair, and his eyes traced my features. He was deep in thought, and I wanted to ask what he was thinking, but I knew he'd come out with it when he was ready.

I felt my eyes growing heavy when Luca lifted up on an elbow. I carved a line between his pectoral muscles with the pad of my thumb. His charcoal eyes were limpid with emotion.

"I could not bear to have you leave again, Delilah," he said.

I scooted closer to him and kissed his chin. "I'm not going anywhere, I promise. I love you. I want to be with you."

"Forever?"

My breath caught. "What? What are you... what are you asking?"

"I'm asking if you wish to be with me, to love me, forever." He took my left hand in his, touched my ring finger. "I do not have anything to glitter here, in this moment. I have only me. Only my love, for all of my life."

I reached up and wrapped a lock of his hair around my ring finger. "Say it, Luca. Say the words."

"Will you be married to me, *mia bella* Delilah?"

I nodded and kissed him. "I will."

Luca laughed. "I suppose this was not the kind of romantic proposal of marriage a woman imagines, hmm?"

"No, probably not, but it was perfect."

"I will buy you a ring, *amore*," Luca said. "Just as soon as we get back to Firenze—"

"Shut up, Luca," I said. "You're spoiling the moment. I don't need a ring. I had one, a big one, and it didn't mean shit. Love me forever, and never betray me. That's all I need."

"This I can do. But I will still buy you a ring, so all the jealous men will know you belong to me."

I snuggled close to him and felt his breathing slow. "I belong to you." I was more tasting the words for myself than saying them to him.

He murmured something unintelligible in Italian, and then he was snoring.

I waited until he was deeply asleep to start my clickity-clacking on the keys.

He's stirring now, and I know he can feel me awake. He wants me to cuddle close to him, and now that I've gotten all this out, I can finally fall asleep.

I said yes.

Oh, boy.

August 3

There was a crazy flurry of activity over the last few days. Apparently getting engaged is a huge deal in Luca's family. We haven't even talked about when we're actually getting married (*gulp*), and already Luca's sisters and sisters-in-law are making plans and taking me away for girl's nights and all sorts of nonsense. There was a huge party when Luca and I announced our news. There was lots of wine and grappa, kids dancing to music played by Elisabetta and Lucia.

They've welcomed me with open arms. They are my family.

August 4

Luca bought me a ring. It's a thin platinum band with two small diamonds to either side of a larger one. It's beautiful, and perfect. He took me to Ponte Vecchio late in the evening, stopped with my back to the railing, crowds passing around us, watching.

He dropped to his knee, a ring box in his hand.

I tugged on him, laughing. "I already said yes, Luca! What are you doing?"

He grinned. "It did not seem correct to just hand it to you. It is an engagement ring. A man must do it right, no? So. Delilah Flores, will you marry me?"

People had stopped to watch, cheering, whistling, calling out encouragement in Italian and English and German and French.

I waited a few seconds, just to draw out the tension of the moment for the crowd, and then I stepped closer to him, bent down and kissed him.

"Yes." I kissed him again and pulled him to his feet. "You are ridiculous, and I love you."

"You are more ridiculous, and I love you."

The crowd around us went nuts, and we both laughed.

May 4 (the following year)

I started a new diary not long after Luca proposed to me. It just seemed to be a new chapter of my life, and I wanted to commemorate it by starting a new diary. But now I want to come back to this one and put on an addendum.

An epilogue, if you will.

I'm getting married tomorrow. I'm sitting in my hotel room in Venice, dressed for my bachelorette party. They don't call it that here, of course, but that's what it is to me.

I called my parents and told them, well, not everything, but that I was getting married in Italy, to an Italian. My mother hung up on me. I didn't bother calling Leah.

Now, waiting for the girls to come bustling into my room and take me out to get me drunk, I know they are truly my family. Lucia was the first to hug me and brush away my tears when Mother hung up on me. Luca was gone at the time, on a business trip to Viterbo.

The funny thing was that while I was hurt, of course, I wasn't devastated like I would have been, once upon a time. I wasn't even all that surprised. No one seemed all that upset that I'd left, after all. Mother didn't ask where I was, or what had happened with Harry, or if I was okay.

Domenica is teaching me to cook. Domenica is a patient teacher, and I am an eager student, so I am learning well. I can almost make Luca's favorite dish to his liking, although he very seriously has made it clear that he doubts I will ever make it like his mother, and I agree. But I can try.

I never cooked back in the States. We ate out, or we ordered in, or we did something simple, partially frozen or from a kit. We rarely ate together. Here, meals are events, a time to gather and discuss life and spend time with family. The entire family, including Luca and I now, all live within minutes of Domenica and Dante, so there are always people eating in the kitchen, or at the long dining room table. Everyone gathers there on Sundays, and various combinations come at will during the week. It is a place where all are welcome, all the time.

When Luca and I had our first real argument as a couple, about something stupid which I cannot now remember, I stormed out the door of our flat and walked to Domenica's. I had a cup of late night coffee with Domenica, who was still up, as if she knew she would be needed. Luca showed up a while later, beer on his breath and lust in his eyes. He kissed his mother, had a cup of coffee, and acted as if nothing had happened.

When he finally dragged me away from his mother, I was still trying to hold on to my irritation over whatever petty thing we'd spatted about. He just laughed at me, pressed me back against a wall, and kissed me until I had no choice but to melt into his lips. He dragged me home, threw me onto our bed, stripped me of my clothes with greedy fingers, and ravaged me with his tongue until I begged him to stop and let me feel him inside me. He obliged me, sliding up my body, lingering with his mouth on my breast, plunging into me without warning. I gasped, hooked my heels around his back, and curled into him, taking all he had to give and demanding more, harder.

The girls are here, demanding I close my laptop and come party with them.

May 6

What a perfect day. We picked Venice because a lot of Luca's extended family was coming from closer to that city. It was a lovely day, as every day seems to be in this country.

There was no bride's side, groom's side in our chapel. I don't know if this is because that's an exclusively American tradition, or because his family tactfully avoided letting it happen. It didn't matter if I didn't have any family, anyway, because Luca has enough for both of us. His mother and father both come from large families, so the chapel was filled to capacity with chattering, laughing family. Like his immediate family, the extended bunch all welcomed me with open, loving arms, flaming bottle-red hair and all. By the time the holidays and Carnivale came around, I was fluent enough in Italian that no one felt the need to revert to English for my sake. That was when I realized I'd really been truly accepted, I think, that I knew I really belonged.

It was an amazing feeling. I'd never really fit in back in the States, not with my family, not with Harry, not in the cutesy little podunk town. Here, in Firenze, with Domenica and Lorenzo and little Benito and baby Maria and Elisabetta, I belong. I fit. I am home.

The wedding. Focus, Delilah.

Oh, my. The wedding was traditional, sung in Latin, and all the standing up and sitting down. It was beautiful, but short and to the point. The real fun was the reception. It took place in a vineyard not far from Venice, outside in the fiery light of the setting sun. There was a live band playing upbeat music, perfect for dancing to. There were gallons of excellent wine, of course. Food by the tableful. There were easily three times as many people at the reception as the wedding, it seemed. Some people saw the party and just showed up, and they were welcome. It was raucous, rowdy, and wild. It lasted through the night and into the following dawn.

I danced until I was exhausted, drank until I was dizzy, and then ate until the buzz went away, and then did it all over again. Eventually, when the gray light of spreading dawn gave way to the full light of day, people started to fade away in ones and twos, and then at last Luca led me inside to the winery building, where a small apartment was ready for us. We crashed that night. We'd partied hard, and fell asleep in our clothes. We woke up a few hours past noon and took a limo to a local airport.

I'm not really doing justice to any of that, honestly. It was the best day of my life. So many people, all having a joyous time, all in celebration of my marriage. Unlike receptions back in the States, this was a cut-loose affair, a true celebration. No one held back, no one felt a need to behave a certain way, or act appropriately. People got drunk, and had fun. There was no drama, no problems.

Oh, I can't put it all into words.

Luca stole me away whenever he could, pulled me into the rows of grapes and kissed me until I was dizzy from his kisses.

Then, once, well past midnight, when we were both drunk, Luca got the look in his eyes, the one that said he wanted me and he didn't care how he had to get it. I led him into the winery building and up some stairs to a darkened office.

I hiked up my dress, now a more party-appropriate number, and he bent me over the desk, held my hips tight, and took me there, keeping our voices hushed and our cries of climax muffled.

When we reappeared, there were catcalls and bawdy suggestions, some not far from the truth. Once, I would have been mortified, but now I took it in stride, laughed it off as good-natured ribbing.

We're on the plane to the Caribbean for our honeymoon, and Luca is still sending work emails while I write this. He says once we get to our hotel on St. Martin he's taking my netbook away until we get back home to Firenze.

I won't mind. I'll have plenty of memories to fill up new diaries in the years to come.

This is Luca writing this. I have stolen her laptop from her. Someday I will buy her a new computer, but for now she says this one is suitable. I think it is ridiculous to use something so small, but if she likes it, what can I say?

Anyway, I have stolen this to say that she will have so much good times on our honeymoon that she will not need to even think of writing her diary. Always writing, is this one.

I have read this diary of hers, when she not looking. She is reading over my shoulder now and slapping me, thinking she is mad. She knows she is not. I think she is a very talented writer, and perhaps she should make this diary into a book. I am thinking many people will find it good to read, as I do.

The airplane is about to land, and the attendants are telling us to put away electronics. So, for Delilah, I will put the correct words at the finish of her diary, this story of how she fell in love with a dashing, handsome Italian man.

She will write more, I know. But as for this one?

The End

About the Author

JASINDA WILDER is a Michigan native with a penchant for titillating tales about sexy men and strong women. When she's not writing, she's probably shopping, baking, or reading. She loves to travel, and some of her favorite vacations spots are Las Vegas, New York City, and Toledo, Ohio. You can often find Jasinda drinking sweet red wine with frozen berries.

To find out more about Jasinda and her other titles, visit her website: www.JasindaWilder.com.

www.ingramcontent.com/pod-product-compliance
Lightning Source LLC
Chambersburg PA
CBHW022156170626
46807CB00005B/2232